I0737191

The Family Secret

SHARRON LEE

WORKBOOK PRESS LLC
187 E Warm Springs Rd,
Suite B285, Las Vegas, NV 89119, USA

Website: https://workbookpress.com/
Hotline: 1-888-818-4856
Email: admin@workbookpress.com

Ordering Information:
Quantity sales. Special discounts are available on quantity purchases by corporations, associations, and others.
For details, contact the publisher at the address above.

ISBN-13:   978-1-953839-35-0 (Paperback Version)

              978-1-953839-36-7 (Digital Version)

REV. DATE: 10/04/2022

The Family
Secret

Sharron Lee

Chapter 1

Sarah, a petite blonde-haired girl, lay reading a magazine. When a thin brown-haired girl with a patch over one eye and the other one swollen almost shut was wheeled into the hospital room on a gurney. Her face was marred with stitches and bruises. The nurses moved her battered body gently onto the hospital bed arranging her broken leg onto a pillow. One nurse put a pillow behind her head while another nurse gave her a sip of water. The third nurse covered her with a blanket before they all left the room.

A tall dark-haired man with gray at the temples and glasses perched on his nose walked into the room. "Hi, Dr. O'Brien," Sarah said when she saw him.

"Hi, Sarah, I came to introduce you to Jane Evans. Jane, this is Sarah Hawkins. You have a lot in common. You both are pregnant and were beaten up."

"Beaten?" Jane questioned. Her brain felt fussy and confused from the anesthetic and the beating. She couldn't remember what had happened. Who had beaten her up? Why? She didn't have anything of value. She touched her face and felt the long line of stitches that marred her cheek. Then she remembered something and reached for her stomach. She felt the bandage on it and tears welled up in her eyes. "Is…is my baby all right?"

"Your baby is safe right now. You took several kicks to your stomach that ruptured your spleen. We fixed it surgically, but your baby has been under a lot of stress between the beating and the surgery. If you go into labour now the baby's chance of surviving is very low, I need you to promise that you will take it easy."

"I will," Jane said as she laid her hand on her stomach and tried to give a little smile but it hurt.

"You also have a broken leg and a concussion. The leg has been set," Dr. O'Brien said as he took his stethoscope from around his neck. "The concussion will require time to heal."

He listened to Sarah's baby and felt her stomach to see which way the baby was lying. He then did the same to Jane. "Your babies are doing fine so I will leave you to get to know each other," Dr. O'Brien said as he walked out the door.

Before they could say much, a man walked in and set his briefcase on the nightstand and put his policeman's hat down on top of it. "Is your name, Jane Evans?"

"Yes," she said hesitantly.

"I am Sergeant Rick Bartlett," the man said as he showed her his badge. "I would like to ask you some questions about the beating? He pulled a notebook and pen from his pocket and settled himself in the chair near her bed ready to write her responses.

"My memory is…," she said not sure how to describe the confusion of thoughts that filled her mind at that moment.

"Just try to answer my questions."

"OK," Jane said not sure what she could tell the man. Her last clear memory was waking up beside Mark that morning in the burnt-out factory they called home. She wondered if Mark had been beaten up also. Was he somewhere in the hospital wondering where she was?

"Had Mark ever hit you before?"

"Mark!" she exclaimed with a shocked look on her face. "He didn't do this. He loves and protects me. He is the father of my child. He never hit me."

"We have witnesses who saw Mark hitting you."

"I can't believe that Mark did this to me. Why would he?"

"What do you remember?"

"My mind is all mixed up. I remember Mark wanting to buy alcohol. This made me angry because I wanted to have a meal. We argued and I left."

"Where did you go?"

"I went to the garage I go to every morning and got cleaned up."

"What else did you do?"

"Don't remember exactly."

"We have witnesses to your beating"

"Who?"

"Jake and Tillie."

"Had they been drinking because Mark wouldn't hurt me?" Jane said as she couldn't believe that Mark had beaten her up.

"They were both sober. Tillie hid behind some crates when she saw Jake climbing in the dumpster. She figured he was up to no good and didn't want to be a part of it. When Mark came into the alley she got scared because she knew Jake wanted to get back at Mark for his beating last week. Mark hid his bag behind the dumpster and went into the back alley to relieve himself. Jake jumped out of the dumpster grabbed a bottle of rum from Mark's bag and climbed back into it before Mark came around the corner of the building. Mark went to his bag and began frantically looking for the bottle. When he didn't find it there, he started looking around the area for whoever took it," said the policeman as he turned the page of his notebook.

"That is when you entered the alley and announced that you were pregnant. Mark went ballistic. He immediately started screaming at you to lose the baby and started punching you and kicking you. Tillie was scared that Mark was going to kill you because his attack on you was so vicious. She was afraid that if she tried to stop him, Mark would kill her also."

"Why would Mark want to hurt me and his baby?" asked Jane. "He told me he wanted children. I don't understand." Jane took a tissue and wiped tears away and blew her nose. She felt scared and confused.

"Jake was peeking out of the dumpster. He backs up every word of Tillie's story."

"Why didn't Jake stop the beating," asked Jane.

"He was afraid of getting beaten up again by Mark. He told me he is still getting over the beating that Mark gave him the week before when he wouldn't give Mark his bottle of gin. He showed me the bruises he still had on his body. He is not a spring chicken and it is harder for him to heal."

"Mark would be furious about the rum. Did he think I took it?" questioned Jane looking for any reason to explain Mark's actions.

"Jake is blaming himself for your beating, but Tillie said Mark left the alley ranting and raving that he hoped that the beating would make you lose the baby. He wanted no part of raising a child. He never once mentioned the bottle that had disappeared in his ranting."

"Mark told me he wanted children. I thought when I told him, he would get a job and get us a place to live." Jane said, "Isn't that what a man is supposed to do when he gets a girl pregnant?" questioned Jane.

"Mark left you hurt and bleeding in the alley that is not the action of a man who loves you. Tillie was the one who got the building owner to call the police and the paramedics. She didn't leave your side until you were put in the ambulance."

"Tillie is very nice to me. She was the one who told me that I was pregnant. She saw me throwing up in the alley a few days ago. I thought I just had the flu or something."

"She said she would be willing to testify in court that Mark did this to you" said the policeman.

"I…I still don't understand all this. Why would he want to hurt his baby or me? He loves me," Jane said as she rubbed her forehead as a headache was starting over her patched eye.

"Do you remember anything of the beating," asked the detective.

"No…not really," Jane said as an image of a fist coming toward her face flashed across her mind.

"Mark will be going to jail for assault."

"What if I don't press charges against him?" Jane said.

"We can arrest him without you pressing charges against him. As a minor, you will be going into foster care or back to your mother's place. I have already contacted your mother. She said she would be in to see you."

"Just what I need, my mother who called me a tramp coming here to find out that I am pregnant. I am almost sixteen and can take care of myself," Jane said defiantly.

"In the eyes of the law, you are a minor. You have no choice in the matter," he said as he stood up. "Do you have any idea where Mark would go?"

"No," Jane said as she remembered that Mark had hid in the subway tunnels when he beat Jake up. She wondered if that is where he was now, sitting in a dark corner somewhere hungry and shivering from the cold.

"I have to take pictures of your injuries," the detective said as he pulled a camera out of his briefcase. He proceeded to take several pictures of her injuries before he put his camera away. He then pulled a card from his pocket and put it on the night stand saying,

"Call me if you remember anything." He turned and left the room.

Jane nodded not knowing what to believe or what to say. She felt like she was in an emotional whirlwind.

"Are you all right," Sarah said. "Remember you are supposed to keep calm."

Jane blurted out. "Don't you think I should be emotional? I am only pregnant at fifteen with no education and no money. My boyfriend is going to jail, and my living options are foster care or my party loving mother's house where drunken men hit on me. I feel emotional. I am angry, betrayed, scared, sad, uncertain, and confused. What will happen to me and my baby?"

"I know how you feel right now. My boyfriend did this to me as she lifted her broken arm. This was the fifth time that he beat me up. I kept going back because I felt I had nowhere else to go. Then I found out I was pregnant. I can't go back to him now. He would kill me and my baby," Sarah said. "Especially now, that I laid charges against him."

The room fell silent. Minutes ticked by until Sarah broke the silence by saying, "We will need help. It is a big responsibility to raise a child. I can remember my mother working two jobs to feed and clothe my brother and me after my father died of cancer."

"How long ago did he die?" asked Jane as she thought about her own father.

"Seven years ago. I still miss him."

"My father died last year." Tears rolled down her face as she wished he was here to hold her and tell her everything would be all right. "I would never have left home if he was still alive. We were so close. I miss him so much," she sobbed.

"You haven't even finished grieving for him. It took me two years not to start crying when I thought of my father," commented Sarah.

"I was on the streets shortly after his death. I spent most of my time searching for food or begging for money. When I did think of him, I would find a quiet hiding place and cry until I couldn't cry anymore."

"You still have your mother. She will help you."

"I am not sure if she will or not," Jane said as she turned to face Sarah.

"Why won't she?"

"She changed right after my father's death. Now all she can think of is going out with her friends and partying."

"I can't see my mother. My brother won't let me into his home or answer my calls because of my boyfriend and that is where my mother is living. She has Alzheimer's. I haven't seen her in so long she may not even remember who I am." Sarah said with a sigh.

The girls continued talking until their lunch trays came. A full belly and a warm bed seduced Jane into a much-needed nap. Sarah soon followed her example.

Jane woke up first and lay thinking about the baby. Would she be a good mother? Would she even be able to keep her baby? Jane was in deep thought when a well-dressed lady about five feet four inches tall walked into the room. Her gray hair was pulled back in a bun and she had a serious look about her.

Sarah woke up when she heard the woman say, "Hello girls, I am Ruth Jacobson. My job here basically is to get people the help they need to overcome the problems they face. Dr. O'Brien spoke to me about your both so I thought I would drop in and have a chat with you girls. It is apparent that you both have been abused and you are both pregnant. I am going to ask you some questions that I want you to seriously think about."

"First, did you watch what you said or did around your boyfriends because you were afraid, they would get angry?" Ms. Jacobson said as she sat down in the chair beside Sarah's bed.

Sarah spoke up and said, "Yes, every time I mentioned my family he got angry. I stopped talking about them."

"Do you feel that you are the only one who could change him?"

"I thought the baby and I would change Mark. I wanted him to stop drinking and get a job," Jane said.

"Did they say things that made you feel bad about yourself?" asked Mrs. Jacobson.

"He was always criticizing me about everything I did," Sarah said.

"Mark was always saying I was stupid and naive," Jane said quietly.

"Did he cut you off from your friends and family?"

"Yes," Sarah said again.

"If you can answer yes to any of these questions than this person has an abusive personality. His abuse would increase over time especially if he uses drugs and alcohol. You are not responsible for his actions and words."

"But…," Jane began to make an excuse for Mark.

"Did he start by putting you down verbally day after day? Did you start believing what he called you? If your answer was yes, you were being verbally abused."

"I guess…" said Sarah as she shifted her position on the bed.

"Did you become depressed, isolated yourself from others, start having nightmares, difficulty in concentrating, eating disorders, and finally drug or alcohol abuse."

"No but...," Jane started to say.

"I guess I was being verbally abused," Sarah said as she sat thinking about some of the times Bill had called her stupid and clumsy. She would head to the kitchen and eat.

"I would advise that both of you girls to get counselling. I can get you enrolled in a counselling program when you are released from the hospital. Now, if you keep your baby, you can get on Social Assistance until you can get an education or a job. There are agencies that can find you low cost housing, food banks, and used clothes. When you are ready to leave the hospital, come to my office on the first floor and I will give you the addresses and information about these agencies. If you decide to give your baby up, I can give you the name of a reputable adoption agency. When you decide what you are going to do contact me at this number," Mrs. Jacobson said as she handed each girls a card before she left the room.

"Boy, what she said hit home with me," Sarah said. "I want to keep my baby and never be in a relationship like I had with Bill ever again."

"I don't know how I am going to keep my baby. I have a lot to think about."

"My mother always told me to break a big problem down into little bits and make the decisions in the order they need to be made in."

"I guess then my first decision is where I go when I leave here, foster care versus my mother's house. My mother may not want me back with a baby involved."

"Then you will have to ask her, won't you. If she doesn't, your decision is made."

Chapter 2

A scream rang out from the girl's room that night. The night nurse came running into the room to find Sarah frantically pushing the button to get a nurse. Jane was sitting up in bed holding her stomach and rocking back and forth.

"Jane, are you in labour? Should I call the doctor?" questioned the nurse.

"He…he kicked me"

"The baby?" asked the nurse.

"No…the man"

"Honey, you are just having a bad dream. Nothing is going to happen to you here. Lie back and rest before you go into labour," the nurse said as she fluffed Jane's pillow up and got Jane settled back down. The nurse reached to turn the light off over Jane's bed.

"Please, leave the light on," Jane asked as tears streamed down her face.

As soon as the nurse left, Sarah asked, "Are you sure you are all right? Were you reliving the beating? I did for the first few days. Just remember that you are safe here."

Jane didn't feel like talking right then so she told Sarah she was fine and to go back to sleep. Jane turned her back on Sarah and laid there thinking about the dream. She remembered the brown boots that kicked her repeatedly. They were Mark's boots. He had really done this to her. Tears continued running down her face as she quietly cried herself to sleep. She had been in love with him. She thought he had loved her. How could he have done this to her and their baby?

Next morning, the surgeon came in to examine Jane's stomach incision and the damage around her eye. He first looked at her stomach and saw that it was healing nicely. He ordered a nurse to clean and rebandage the incision.

"Now, let us see how that eye is coming. It was a challenge to get the bone back together. He told Jane, "I want you to keep your eyes closed, while I take the bandage off your eye."

"OK," Jane said nervously. She had been worried that her eye was damaged, and she would be blind in it.

"Now, open them slowly because the light may hurt that eye a bit," the doctor said as he removed the patch over the one eye.

Her eye began to water, and her sight was blurry for a few seconds until her eyes focused.

"Tell me how many fingers, I am holding up," the doctor said as he moved his hand around putting a different number of fingers up each time. Jane told him the correct number each time.

"Good," the doctor said. "You still have a lot of swelling and bruising around the eye socket, but it is healing nicely. Unfortunately, you are not so lucky on your cheek. It was torn up badly. You will need some plastic surgery in the future."

"Doctor, can I…ah…look in a mirror?" Jane asked wondering how badly damaged her face was?

"I will get a mirror," the doctor said. When the doctor returned with the mirror, Jane took it not knowing what to expect. No one had mentioned plastic surgery to her before. She was stunned at what she saw. Her face was distorted by swelling and bruises on it. What was worse was the line of stitches that circled the one eye, the line of jagged stitches down her check, and one across her forehead. She had been a pretty girl now she felt like a freak. Tears welled up in her eyes and ran down her cheeks.

"With more healing, your face won't look as bruised and misshaped," the doctor said trying to comfort her.

"I hope so," Jane said as the doctor left.

Sarah said, "Jane, I looked terrible every time Bill beat me up. In a week, you will look a lot different."

"How am I going to pay for plastic surgery?"

"I don't know but you will have it done," Sarah said confidently.

"This just adds to the pile of problems I face. I just want to be left alone so I can think," Jane said as she turned her back on Sarah.

"Ok." Sarah understood all the feelings and fears that Jane was going through. She was going through them herself.

Chapter 3

That evening, Jane's mother walked in. She was wearing an expensive dress with high heels. "Oh, my poor baby, are you all right?" she exclaimed when she saw Jane's face.

Anger welled up inside Jane, "I wouldn't be here if I was all right?" Jane said sarcastically.

"I have been so worried about you."

"You were so worried that it took you two days to get here. Most parents would come immediately to their child's bed side. It shows me just how much you care."

"But I had to work," her mother said defensively.

"Work should not stop a parent coming to their child's hospital bed. You certainly weren't worried when that sleaze ball propositioned me. You didn't believe one word I said to you that night. You chose to listen to the dirty old man, over your own daughter. You cared so much you kicked me out of the house. I wouldn't be here if you cared." Jane's resentment and anger burst to the surface like a volcano spewing lava.

"I know I was wrong and owe you an apology. I was afraid because the guy threatened to sue us for slander. I was drunk and didn't think that you would leave. I didn't realize you were gone until the next morning. After your father died, I just felt so lost and alone, I went looking for companionship. Everyone was drinking so I drank to be accepted. I have a job now and friends who golf and do things other than drink constantly. I have changed."

"Good, I want the mother I loved back," Jane said firmly.

"Oh, honey, I am so sorry." Her mother gave her a hug and a kiss on her forehead.

"Why didn't you try to find me?" Jane was still not sure whether she believed her mother or not. She felt it would take a long time for her to trust her mother again.

"I reported you missing to the police and even hired a private detective to find you. What else could I do? Please, please forgive me," begged her mother. "I want you to come home."

"Mom, I have to tell you that there is a baby involved."

"A baby, where is it?"

"I am pregnant," Jane said in a low voice. She felt ashamed because her father always expected more from her.

"We need to get you well then we can worry about what to do with the baby."

"I would like to keep the baby if I can."

"You are only fifteen years old and a baby is a life changing occurrence. You have a lot to consider so don't make your mind up so soon," advised her mother. "Take time to think everything through first that is all I am saying."

"Ok."

"Good"

"You want me to come home but if I do, I want to be able to contact you if I need you."

"I am an adult. I don't have to report to you," her mother said sternly.

"I want this in case I go into labour. You want to be there don't you when your grandchild is born?"

"Oh…of course, I do,"

Jane grabbed her stomach and let out a loud "Ow…" as a sharp pain flashed across it.

Sarah, who had been listening to every word while pretending to read a magazine, hit her bell and a nurse rushed in. "Is everything, okay?"

"Jane just had a pain," Sarah exclaimed.

The nurse called for Dr. O'Brien on the intercom. He rushed in to examine Jane. He ordered that she be given a shot to relax her. He then ushered Jane's mother out of the room as he explained to her that stress could cause Jane to lose the baby. Jane soon fell into a deep sleep.

Chapter 4

Jane woke up early the next morning. Sarah was still sleeping so she laid thinking about what her mother had said. She had to decide to either go home or go into foster care.

Finally, Sarah rubbed her eyes and stretched.

"Sarah, what are you going to do when you leave the hospital?"

"My neighbour knew I was pregnant and had seen me the last time I was beaten up. She feared for my safety when she heard us fighting. She called the police. When I heard the sirens, I told Bill I was going to press charges this time. I wasn't going to let him hurt me or the baby ever again. When he heard the police car screech to a stop in front of the apartment building, he ran. The police put me in touch with the counsellor at the women's shelter. I am going to go there when I get out of the hospital. They are going to help me get back on my feet."

"Do you think Bill will come after you?"

"Yes, he threatened to kill me."

"Aren't you scared?"

"Terrified but I have to do this for the sake of my baby," as she rolled on her side and faced Jane. "When Mrs. Jacobson talked to us, I realized that Bill was killing me slowly. I was living in constant fear of angering him. That is no way to live. I want an education, a job, and a loving home where I can raise my child."

"When I first landed on the street, I tried to find a job but no one would hire a minor with no identification."

"You have nothing saying who you are?"

"No, I had never needed identification other than a student card," Jane said as she shifted her position in the bed. "I guess I will need identification to establish a home for my baby."

"I think you will need it to get Social Assistance," Sarah said. "We can find out at the library or go the Social Assistance office uptown."

"We…what do you mean we," Jane asked.

"Last night while you were sleeping, I was thinking it would be nice to have a friend who knows what you are going through. We can face the challenges together," Sarah smiled at Jane. "Maybe we can establish a home together then we can help each other get things like our high school diplomas."

"You haven't got your diploma. I thought since you were older you would have it."

"No, I dropped out of school to be a full-time housewife like Bill wanted. I did everything to please him," Sarah said shaking her head.

"I was crazy staying with him."

"I still have to make the decision whether to go into foster care or go back home with my mother. I am leaning towards going home but I know she will try to get me to give up my baby."

"When my mother got sick my brother and his wife took us in. I hated living with them. I felt like their servant cleaning up after the children and babysitting their children or mother. I was so excited about moving in with Bill. When I was at his place, we had always cooked together and did chores together. I thought that would continue when I moved in. It didn't. Bill sat on his fanny and ordered me to do everything. When it wasn't the way he wanted it done, he would hit me."

"Why didn't you go back to your brother's place?"

"My brother was furious when I moved out. He told me I wasn't welcome in his home ever again if I went with Bill. I didn't know what to do when the beatings started. I felt stupid and ashamed that I hadn't listened to my brother's warnings and I didn't know if he would forgive me on one hand. On the other hand, I was afraid Bill would kill me if I tried to leave so I stayed."

"I thought that I had it bad. I just had to battle off drunks and perverts. If I go back there, I just want to feel safe in my room."

"You can. Buy a barrel bolt from the hardware store and put it on your door and your door frame. When you are in your room you can lock yourself in. We used them when mother started getting up and wandered out of the house in the middle of the night with her Alzheimer's."

"That sounds like a good idea. How much are they?"

"I don't remember exactly but I think they were only a few dollars."

A nurse walked in holding a cold pitcher of water. "Do you girls need more water?"

"I would like some," Jane said as she held up her glass for the nurse to refill. "Could you get us a pen and some paper to write on?"

"I will see what I can find." Shortly, the nurse returned with a note pad and a pink pen that said, "It's a girl."

"What is that for?" Sarah asked.

"Let's make a list of things we need to do to keep our babies and a list of the things we need for them," Jane said as she began writing down identification for herself. She finally felt like she was taking a step to keep her baby.

"We will have to contact Social Assistance," Sarah said with a smile on her face.

"We need to find out how to complete high school and what college courses we will need to take."

"What would you like to be?" questioned Sarah as she turned on her back and looked up at the ceiling.

"I always wanted to be a teacher, but I don't know if I will ever get there now," Jane said sadly.

"Working together, we can do it. I want to be a nurse. It will be hard work for both of us but if we help each other, we can reach our dreams," Sarah said confidently.

"United we stand. Divided we fall," Jane mumbled as her father's favorite saying crossed her mind.

"We will have to get health cards, social insurance cards, set up bank accounts, get insurance, and make wills. I left my bank card and all my things at the apartment, but I definitely am not going back there without a body guard."

Suddenly, Jane realized that all these things were what adults needed. Was she mature enough to handle all this responsibility? She had never even held a baby before. "I have a lot of questions to ask about my pregnancy, the delivery, and later about taking care of a baby." Jane said as she wondered how painful her delivery would be.

"My mother can't remember me half of the time so I can't ask her any questions. Have you ever asked your mother about her pregnancy with you?"

"Strange now that you mention it, my mother has never mentioned anything about when she was expecting me. I wonder why?" Jane frowned. "Maybe, Dr. O'Brien will talk to us about what to expect."

"Did I hear my name," Dr. O'Brien said as he walked in and pulled up a chair between their beds. "What tomfoolery are you two young ones up to? I heard you wanted a pad of paper and a pen. Are you two planning a hospital break?" he said with a big grin on his face.

"We were thinking that if we shared an apartment and helped each other we could keep our babies. Does that sound like a good plan?"

"It does as long as you can stand each other's moods. Your hormones are bouncing all over the place so you will have two moody characters under the same roof right now."

"We will remember that when we are living together," giggled Sarah.

"We have some courses given by hospital staff about pregnancy and taking care of the babies afterwards. Would you like to enroll in these classes?"

"Don't they cost money?" questioned Jane.

"They usually do but I talked to the instructors about you two. They are willing to enroll you free. These courses will help you both make an informed decision on what is best for you and your babies."

"I think I would like to take the courses," Jane said. "I know very little about babies."

"I know about taking care of kids but we are a team so I will take the courses with you." Sarah said with a smile.

"Good," Dr. O'Brien said as he put the chair back against the wall. "I will get your both enrolled and the information on when the classes start."

A few hours later, Jane's mother came in. She again was dressed in an expensive suit. She had had her hair done. "I can't spend a lot of time with you tonight. I have a date. I just wanted to tell you that I love you and want the best for you. I will go along with whatever you decide to do about the baby," she said as she patted Jane's hand.

"They tell me you can come home in a few days. Your room is exactly how you left it. It is there waiting for you. Remember I love you, but I must go. My date is waiting in the parking lot. See you tomorrow," Jane's mother said as she disappeared out the door.

Chapter 5

When Jane was released from the hospital, she felt nervous about going home with her mother. Her mother had only spent an hour or less a day with her at the hospital and most of that time was spent with her trying to point out to Jane every reason she should give her baby up. Even though she had said she would live with Jane's decision.

When Jane saw the grey brick home she grew up in, she wondered if it would ever be the place that meant security, love, and happiness to her like it had when her father was alive. As they pulled into the driveway, Jane noticed that the garage and her father's workshop looked neglected. Paint was peeling off the building and weeds were growing up around it. If her father was alive, he would be upset that his favorite place was so neglected.

She maneuvered her crutches carefully as she went up the front steps to the house excited to see the beautiful wood furniture her father had made and the soft fluffy couch that seemed to hug her when she sat on it. She was shocked when she entered the house. The warm living room she loved was gone. In its place, was a super modern living room filled with glass and chrome furniture. The walls were a stark white with abstract black and white paintings scattered about the room. The floor was covered by a black rug in front of a long black cabinet. The largest flat screen television Jane had ever seen was suspended on the wall above the cabinet.

"Isn't this beautiful? I decorated it myself using a picture out of one of my magazines," her mother exclaimed as she kicked off her shoes and put them in the front closet.

Jane was at a loss for words. Her mother seemed so proud of it.

She stammered, "Err…yes, it is very modern and hip," as she kicked off her one shoe and put it in the closet.

"I have to get ready for work, honey," her mother said as she headed to her bedroom.

Jane wandered around the rest of the house to see what other changes had been made. The dining room now held a chrome and glass table with ultra-modern chairs. The kitchen now had stainless steel appliances and a new granite counter top on new shiny white cabinets. Jane wondered where her mother had gotten the money to do all this.

Jane went down the hall to her bedroom. She was anxious to see all the cherished items that she had to leave behind when she left. When she opened the door, Jane became confused. Her mother had said she had not changed her room? Yet this room was not the same as she remembered it.

She remembered yellow walls, but these walls were pink. Her desk had been beside the closet. Now her bed was there. Even her patterned bedspread was pink now instead of yellow. Was her memory playing a trick on her?

She slowly moved around the room touching different items. Her angel doll stood on the dresser. She remembered holding it all through her childhood whenever she was upset. She took it in her arms and held it tight to her chest as she continued walking around her room. She stopped to look at her Jonas Brothers' poster remembering her father standing among a mob of screaming teeny boppers in front of the stage. He had taken her to the concert for her birthday. He hated the music, but he had done it for her. She picked up one of her trophies. Her father had never missed one of her races. He was so proud of her when she won that trophy for the hundred-yard dash. She had done her best time ever in that race and had set a new school record. She lay down on the bed with her angel and cried.

"Jane, I am leaving for work. I will bring something home for dinner around six o'clock. Get some rest," her mother called out as she left for work.

"Ok," Jane responded as she grabbed a Kleenex and blew her nose.

She got up and wandered around the house wondering what her mother had done with the old furniture. She had always hoped that the pieces her father made would be hers someday. She remembered the smell of lemon oil her father used on the wood. Why did her mother get rid of her father's things?

She finally decided to call Sarah who had moved into the women's shelter two days before.

"Jane are you home?" when she was called to the phone.

"Yes, but everything has changed."

"What do you mean?"

"Our once cozy living room is now a super modern magazine picture. What is even stranger is that my mother said she had not touched my room, but it is not the same as I remember."

"What is different?"

"The walls are pink instead of yellow and the furniture is rearranged."

"Are you sure? You are still experiencing memory loss. Maybe you are remembering what your bedroom looked like years ago. Do you have pictures anywhere that you can look at?"

"I didn't think of my photo album. It is full of pictures of me and my friends all over the house. I will go and find it and call you back."

"I will be waiting for your call."

Jane hobbled to her room and found her photo album in the bottom drawer of her dresser where she had always kept it. She sat down on her bed and leafed through it. She didn't find one picture that matched her memory of her room. Every picture had pink walls and the furniture where it is now. Why would she remember her room one way when it was never that way? This question nagged at her as she sat on the bed looking at the album for over an hour. She jumped when the phone rang.

"Jane, why didn't you call me back?" Sarah anxiously asked.

"I didn't realize the time. I am confused. The room is the same as it is now in all the pictures. I don't understand. Why is my memory different?" Jane muttered.

Maybe the concussion you received has just scrambled your memory and with rest it will change. Maybe talking to the counsellor here tomorrow will help. You are coming to the group meeting here, aren't you?"

"Yes, I think maybe I should talk to someone."

"Good, I will see you tomorrow."

Jane felt very agitated. She wondered if rest would help her as she headed back into her bedroom. She tried to rest but her mind would not shut down. She finally went to the kitchen for a drink of milk. The phone rang as she was putting her dirty glass into the dishwasher. She went to the living room and picked it up. There was only a dial tone. She just thought that she had been too slow in answering it.

She turned on the television and sat the phone on the table beside her. A few minutes later, the phone rang again. Jane picked it up immediately and all she heard was a dial tone. That is strange, she thought. She didn't think any more of it until she received three more of these phone calls. Why would someone call and then just hang up?

At six, her mother walked in with hamburgers and French fries.

While they were eating, her mother announced that she was going out on a date. Jane thought she would be fine even though the phone calls had unsettled her a bit.

Jane lay on the couch after her mother left watching television. She had just got interested in a movie when she heard a knock at the back door. Who could that be, she wondered as she headed for the back door? When she got there, no one was there. She looked out the windows in the kitchen and she didn't see anyone. Was her mind playing tricks on her? She was sure that the knock had come from the back door. Could it have been the front door? She went to the front door and peeked out the peep hole. She couldn't see anyone. She was sure she had heard a knock on a door. What was going on with her?

She went back to her seat and watched the movie a few minutes when the lights started flicking on and off. Yet the television didn't flicker. How is that possible she wondered? Was she seeing things?

As the night progress, she jumped up several times when she heard knocking on the front or back door. Each time no one was there. Were these things really happening or was she imagining all this? She didn't know what to believe. She decided that maybe she did need to rest so she went to bed and curled up with her angel doll. Sleep didn't come easily. She kept hearing noises that she could not explain. Something being dragged across the floor; animal's nails scurrying across the floor; someone speaking but she could not make out the words. Why were these things happening? Was her mind playing tricks on her? Had she incurred brain damage when she was beaten up? These questions swirled around her brain until exhaustion set in and she fell asleep.

Chapter 6

The next morning, her mother sat in her shabby pink housecoat with her hair up in large curlers drinking coffee at the table when Jane entered the kitchen. The radio was playing country music in the background. Jane was wearing gray sweat pants and a yellow tee shirt. She sat and ate cereal listening to her mother tell her about her date the night before.

She just got up to rinse her cereal bowl and put it in the dishwasher when the phone rang. It was on the table beside her mother who didn't make any attempt to answer it. After the fifth ring, Jane dried her hands and reached for the phone. Her mother looked at her with an odd expression on her face. Jane put the phone to her ear and there was only a dial tone.

As Jane put the phone back on the table, her mother said, "Why did you pick up the phone? It didn't ring?"

"I…thought I heard it," Jane stuttered wondering what was going on. She was positive she had heard it.

"It didn't ring. One sign of concussion is ringing in your ears. Is that what you heard? If so, you better tell the doctor."

"That…must be what I heard." Jane felt sick at her stomach? She quickly straightened the kitchen. "I think I will go and lay down," Jane said as she left the room. Jane hurried to her room and sat on her bed pondering what had happened. Was the concussion causing all these strange things to happen? What did you do to cure a concussion? Why didn't the doctors not seem to be very worried about the concussion? Was it worse than a concussion, like brain damage? All these worries ran around in Jane's mind until she heard the front door close and her mother's car drive away.

She hurried into the living room and peeked out the window

making sure her mother had left for work. Jane searched the bookcase for the medical book her mother swore by. When she found it, she looked up concussions? It said that some people will have continuous buzzing in their ears. This didn't describe her hearing. She was hearing distinct sounds not continual buzzing.

Jane jumped when the phone rang beside her. She hesitantly reached for it letting it ring several times expecting it to stop ringing. It didn't stop until she finally picked it up. Sarah was on the line. Jane let out a sigh of relief.

"What took you so long to answer?"

"Err…I was in the bathroom," Jane lied.

"Are you feeling up to coming to the meeting today?"

"Yes, what time is the meeting?" Jane said wanting any excuse to get away from the house and around other people. These strange things didn't happen while she was in the hospital. Did it mean she needed more rest?

"It starts at eleven o'clock but come early so we can visit. I haven't left this place because of Bill and I am going stir crazy. I will tell the counsellor that you will be coming so you will be let in."

"I want to stop at the hardware store. I found four dollars and eighteen cents in an old change purse of mine. I hope that is enough to get that barrel bolt. I will get there as soon as I can."

Jane went to the kitchen to get a glass of milk before she left. When she opened the refrigerator door, there was no milk. That is strange. There was almost a full container of milk when she had breakfasted this morning. It wasn't on the counter or table, so she started looking in the cupboards. She found it sitting beside the cereal bowls. She was confused. She was sure that she had put it in the refrigerator. Had she put it in the cupboard instead? She had been the one who cleaned up the breakfast dishes and cleared the table.

As she hobbled down the street on her crutches, her mind was in a turmoil. Jane was scared that she had brain damage. How else could she explain everything that had happened? How was she going to tell Sarah? Would Sarah still want to be her friend if she was not mentally stable?

She was led into the common room at the women's shelter.

Sarah jumped up when she saw Jane and gave her a hug. "I have missed talking to you. Did you get something for your bedroom door?"

"Oh, yea…ah," Jane stammered as she realized that she had forgotten all about going to the hardware store.

"Ladies, the meeting will start in twenty minutes," the counsellor said as she opened the doors of the meeting room. The girls went in and found their seats and talked as the room filled with women of all different ages all showing signs of abuse. The counsellor asked each one to tell how they were abused. Jane felt embarrassed and uncomfortable when it was her turn, but Sarah encouraged her. The counsellor told them that the beating was not caused by something they had done. It was caused because the men involved didn't know how to control or express their anger in an acceptable way. They were worse when they used drugs or alcohol.

The counsellor worked with each lady on ways to boost their confidence. They worked on ways to combat the fear that many of them felt in what they thought were threatening situations. Jane tried to listen but her mind kept straying to the things that had happened and her fear that her mind was damaged.

After the meeting, the girls asked the counsellor about their plan and ways to accomplish the things they wanted to do. All the while, Jane was distracted, and Sarah noticed it.

"Jane, what is bothering you?"

Jane sat there looking at her hands wondering what to say.
"Come on, what has happened?"

"I am hearing ringing when the phone hasn't rung," Jane blurted out.

"That is no big deal. A friend I had in school was in a car accident. After that she had ringing in her ears constantly. It didn't hurt her at all." Sarah gave Jane a hug. "You will be fine."

"I hope so," Jane said as the fear of losing Sarah as her friend if she had brain damage crossed her mind. "I better get going." Jane began grabbing her belongings and stood up ready to leave. I didn't tell mother I was coming here, and she will be home from work soon."

"Yes, I have washing to do, and I have to take my turn helping with supper tonight." Sarah said as they walked to the door. "I will call you later."

"Ok," Jane said as she left the woman's shelter. On the way home, she stopped at the hardware store and picked up the dead bolt. She couldn't wait to get it installed. That feeling was intensified when she entered the living room. All the furniture was rearranged and sat on a red rug. Even the paintings had changed from black to red. She closed her eyes and shook her head as if trying to shake this color change from her head. She then slowly opened one eye and peeked at the furnishing. The rug and paintings were still red, and the furniture had been rearranged. Had her mother done this?

She heard the squeak of the kitchen's back door as it closed. "Mom, are you home?" Jane called. No one answered. She took her crutch and held it ready to swing it like a club as she hobbled into the kitchen. No one was there. The back door was locked, and no one was in the back yard. Had she imagined the noise?

Jane sat for a few minutes wondering how to explain the changes. Who would do all this? It had to be her mother. She decided to see if her mother had gotten off work early but when her mother answered her work phone and Jane heard the store's

PA system in the background Jane didn't know what to think.
"Why are you calling? Are you all right?

"Oh, I…err…wondered what you wanted for dinner," Jane blurted out trying to cover her confusion.

"I will bring something home. I have a meeting to go to tonight."

"Oh…ok," Jane said as she cringed at the thought of another night alone in the house.

Two hours later her mother came in. She dropped her purse and the take-out food on a table in the living room that had not been by the front door the day before. She kicked her shoes off and carried the food into the kitchen. Jane watched wondering when her mother would notice the changes in the living room.

"Jane, dish out the food. All I want to do right now is to sit down with my feet up and drink a cold beer. Everything went wrong at work today." She grabbed a beer from the refrigerator and headed back into the living room. She turned on the television and sat down on the lounge chair. She never mentioned anything about the rearranged furniture or the changed colours.

Jane didn't know what to think. Was she imagining all the changes? Why didn't her mother notice the bright red rug? Why didn't she notice the table was in a different place? Nothing was making sense to Jane.

Jane came into the living room and handed her mother a dish of Chinese food. They ate in silence watching a game show. Then her mother went to get cleaned up for the meeting while Jane cleaned up the dirty dishes. She sat in the living room with the television on. She pretended to watch it but instead she was lost in her thoughts. She now was hearing and seeing things. How was she going to tell Sarah? She didn't want to lose her friendship. Without Sarah, Jane didn't think she had enough strength to stand up against her mother's desire for Jane to give her baby away.

After her mother left, the phone started ringing. Jane answered and no one was on the line. This happened several times until finally Jane didn't even bother answering it. The lights flicked on and off several times and she heard noises in different areas of the house but when she investigated no one was there. She checked all the windows, closets, and doors to make sure she was alone in the house. She then installed the barrel bolt and locked herself in her room with the medical book trying to find an explanation for what was going on around her.

Chapter 7

Jane woke up the next morning, still dressed lying on top of her bedspread holding her angel doll in her arms. The house was silent. She wandered into the kitchen looking for her mother. Instead she found a note that read:

Jane,

I have gone golfing with friends. Then I have a meeting at the Club and a dinner date tonight. There is a protein drink for you in the refrigerator. Stir it before you drink it. The drink will give you all the minerals and vitamins your baby needs.

Mom

She was alone again. She got the drink out of the refrigerator and stirred it like her mother had said. As she sipped the drink, she made faces because it was a little bitter. She rinsed the glass out and went into the living room. Everything was back in their original positions and the room was again black and white. What was going on? She had not left the house. Wouldn't she have heard someone moving the furniture around? She jumped when the phone rang bringing her mind back from the scary thoughts that were starting to plague her. She hesitantly picked up the phone.

"What took you so long to answer the phone? I am going stir crazy here. Do you want to start on our list today? I have to get my life straightened around soon," said Sarah.

"What do you have in mind?" Jane said anxiously. The fear of losing Sarah's friendship filled her mind. Sarah treated her like she was normal, but she didn't know about the things that were happening around her. Would Sarah want to be around her if she had brain damage of some kind? She knew she had to tell Sarah what was happening.

"Let's go to the library and see what we need to get out birth certificates and social insurance numbers."

"Don't we need money for that?"

"Only a few dollars to print off the forms we need."

"I only have thirty-five cents,"

"I stashed some money away that Bill didn't know about. When I learned I was pregnant, I did odd jobs while he was at work so I could leave him if he threatened the baby.

"I need to earn some money."

"You are supposed to take it easy, so you don't lose your baby."

"I know. When do you want to meet?"

"Can you be at the library in an hour?"

"I think so."

"I will see you there." Sarah said and hung up the phone.

Jane quickly showered and dressed. When she left the house, she didn't notice the man in a gray jacket and blue jeans who followed her. She was so deep in thought of how to tell Sarah about the things happening around her.

She approached the large brick building when Sarah stepped out of a small alcove near the front door. "Oh, you startled me," Jane exclaimed.

"Follow me, I feel exposed out here." Sarah said as she hurried into the building. "Last night, the police accompanied me to the apartment to get my belongings. Bill had emptied the apartment out except for my possessions which he shredded and broke into a million pieces. The only thing I saved was my stash under a loose floor board in the spare bedroom."

"That is scary. Shouldn't you stay at the Women's Centre until he is arrested?"

"I lived in fear of him for two years. I must break the cycle of abuse by standing up to the fear and take my life back. To do that I have to get all my identification replaced."

"I have to tell…" Jane started to say.

"There is a free computer," Sarah interrupted Jane as she hurried to the empty chair in front of the machine and sat down. She turned on the machine and began searching for the forms they needed. Jane started to tell Sarah about what was going on with her several times but each time she started Sarah would interrupt her by asking for an answer to one of the questions on the forms. Finally, Jane gave up and thought she would talk to Sarah after she was done. Twenty minutes later Sarah handed Jane some forms.

Jane looked at them and lamented, "Where am I going to get eighty dollars? I need a job."

"Are you sure that you don't have a birth certificate somewhere?"

"I don't ever remember seeing it."

"Did you ever remember travelling out of Canada?"

"We went to Disneyland when I was about eight years old."

"Then you have a birth certificate somewhere. Oh," Sarah exclaimed as she glanced at her watch. "I have to leave. I must sign the new charges against Bill. See you later."

Sarah grabbed her forms and hurried away leaving Jane standing there.

Jane still hadn't had the chance to tell Sarah what was going on around her. She picked up the forms and left the library and slowly walked home. She again was so wrapped up in her thoughts she didn't notice the man that was watching her.

When she stepped in the house, her mother was sitting in the living room with a frown on her face. "Where have you been? I have been worried sick. I didn't know if you were rushed to the hospital or if you ran away again."

"I just went to the library. I thought you were going to be gone all day."

"Change of plans. If you wanted books to read why didn't you tell me? I would have picked some up for you." Jane's mother said just as she noticed Jane was not carrying any books. "Where are they?"

"I went to use the computer," Jane said holding up the forms she had in her hand.

"Why?"

"To get information about getting a birth certificate and a social insurance number, I need them to get Social Assistance after the baby is born."

"No child of mine will be going onto Assistance. How would I explain that to my friends? I am not going to be embarrassed by you again. Just explaining about the baby is embarrassment enough. I told them you were raped when you were visiting your aunt in Toronto. I had already told them when you left that you were visiting your aunt," her mother said as she grabbed the forms from Jane's hand and ripped them into small pieces.

"You told them a lie," exclaimed Jane.

"I sure did. I was not going to tell them that you were living on the street and got yourself pregnant by an abusive boyfriend."

Jane was furious. "How dare you tell your friends lies to make yourself look good? You put me on the street," Jane screamed as she hurried to her bedroom slamming the door and locking it. Jane threw herself on her bed and cried. She had to keep her baby and get out of this house. To do this she needed three things; money, her birth certificate, and a social insurance number.

She had to get a job and she had to search for her identification. She finally came up with a plan to make up flyers that she could give out to the neighbours. Maybe they had some easy jobs she could do for money.

After her mother left the house, Jane made some pancakes to eat and cleaned up. She set to work making flyers to put in the neighbour's mailboxes. She went on a walk around the neighborhood putting the flyers in the different mail boxes in the area. When she got back, her leg was hurting. She sat down on the lounge chair in the back yard. It was not long before the heat of the sun, the sound of the wind in the trees and the occasional song of a bird lulled Jane into a deep sleep. She didn't wake up until she heard a lawn mower approaching her.

"Excuse me. I hate to disturb you, but I must get this lawn cut for Mrs. Evans. My name is Chuck," the tall dark-haired man said who stood beside her chair.

"I am Jane, Mrs. Evan's daughter."

"I can move your chair to an area I have cut, and you can continue lounging in the sun."

"I think I got enough sun for one day," Jane said as she got up and headed for the back door of the house. Jane felt uncomfortable because Chuck did not take his eyes off her. In one way, she felt flattered especially since she felt fat and unattractive at this stage of her pregnancy. In another way, why would an older man be interested in a girl who was not sixteen yet? That thought made her feel creepy.

When Jane stepped into the kitchen, she was faced with a mess. There were broken eggs and their shells scattered over the counters.

Milk dripped off the counter onto the floor in a huge puddle, and flour was everywhere. Who had done this?

"Mom, are you home?" No one answered. She had made pancakes earlier, but she had cleaned up after herself. Hadn't she? She thought she had worked only on the kitchen island. How did the ingredients get all over the floor and kitchen? Jane began cleaning the mess up before her mother returned and saw it. Had she done this and not remembered?

Chapter 8

The next morning, Jane visited the neighbors and found a few small jobs to make money. She did not tell her mother or Sarah about the jobs. She did not feel like arguing with them about what strenuous work was defined as. Jane knew she would have to be careful, but she was doing this to keep her baby. She had to make money to get her identification if she could not find her birth certificate and her social insurance number in the house somewhere.

Every morning she drank the drink her mother prepared her. She would then meet Sarah for the group therapy at the women's shelter. She felt it was helping her cope with her feelings and the nightmares that abused women sometimes go through, but nothing helped her understand the strange occurrences happening at her home. Every day she was finding things in odd places when she was sure she had put them in the right places. Many items had changed color and then returned to its original color in the weeks that had passed. Her mother used every opportunity to try to convince Jane to give the baby up. All the time she wondered if she would be an unfit mother. Jane began to doubt herself more and more.

Guilt plagued her because she had not told Sarah about these occurrences. Sarah was making all kinds of plans about when they could move in together. Yet Jane feared that she might endanger the children if she was around them doing these crazy things. The only time, Jane felt normal was when she was with Sarah. Why did nothing odd happen when she was with her? Jane could not bear the thought of losing Sarah's friendship. So, she kept quiet about what was happening to her.

The girls were also attending the classes Dr. O'Brien had enrolled them in. They were amazed to learn that their babies already had hair and nails. When they saw ultrasound pictures of their babies, Sarah's baby was sucking its thumb and Jane's baby had her eyes open looking at them. Every day they were realizing more and more that they had another human being growing inside them.

One day after class, Sarah stayed at the hospital for her appointment with Dr. O'Brien. Jane walked to the corner store to pick up milk her mother asked her to get. She was standing at the cooler when three of her old friends walked in laughing and giggling.

"John is going to the beach party tonight," Connie said with a dreamy smile on her face.

"He is so cute, but he will be with June," Becky gave a big sigh.

"No, he won't. Didn't you two read the text I sent you last night?" said Barb. "They broke up last night at the movies. She slapped his face and everything before she marched out of the movie. Everyone there saw it."

"I just bought a new bikini and cover up," said Connie. "I hope he notices me. I have had a crush on him since before Jane was going with him. Did you hear about Jane?"

Jane had not thought about John in a long while. They had gone to the movies a few times together just before she left home. Now he was the farthest thing from her mind. When she heard her name, she strained to hear every word that was said.

"Yes, I heard that she was raped and is now pregnant. Wouldn't it be terrible to carry a baby of a rapist?" Connie said as she approached the cooler where Jane stood. "Oh my," exclaimed Connie when she realized it was Jane standing there.

Jane didn't know what to say. Should she tell them the truth or leave the lie alone? So, she turned to the girls and said, "Yes, I am between six and seven months pregnant now?"

"We are a…going to a beach party tonight so we are …picking up some snacks to bring," Connie stammered trying to cover up her shock at all the scars on Jane's face. "All…the gang is uh…going to be ah…there. Would you um…like to come?"

"No, my leg is already itching with this cast on. Imagine how itchy it would be with sand in it. Plus, right now my figure is not the best for a bikini," Jane said trying to cover up the awkwardness she felt. "Besides with all these scars on my face, most of the gang wouldn't recognize me."

"Ok, later then," Connie quickly turned and walked out with the other girls. They each took one last look and then exited the building whispering to each other.

Jane paid for the milk and left the store. As she walked home her thoughts turned to her old friends. She realized that even if she gave the baby up for adoption, she would never be one of her gang again. She was no longer that innocent giggling immature fifteen-year-old girl. She was soon going to be a mother and if she was going to keep her baby she had to start acting like an adult.

As she walked home, she didn't notice the man following her again.

When she came in the front door, things had changed. The chrome and glass furniture were now sitting on a bright yellow carpet and the paintings were now multicolored. She didn't know what to do or think. Was everything just black and white like normal and only she saw the colour or was these things really a different colour?

When her mother came home, she didn't say one word about the color changes in the room. Jane accepted it thinking that she was hallucinating. She would have to tell someone soon about all the things that have happened for the safety of her baby, but she kept hoping that she would come up with an explanation. She didn't want to accept the idea that she had brain damage. She was happy however when her mother announced that she was staying in. Maybe she could muster up enough courage to tell her mother what was going on.

At dinner, Jane announced that she had chosen Sarah to be her delivery coach.

"What!" her mother exploded. "Why would you choose a total stranger? I should be your delivery coach. You don't need her in the delivery room. I will be there."

"I am sorry. I thought since I was her delivery coach. I should have her as mine. Also, she has the time to take the course, which is running when you are working." Jane tried to explain why she had asked Sarah.

"Make sure you tell that girl that I will be there as your coach not her," her mother yelled and stomped out of the room.

Jane didn't know what to do. She wanted Sarah to be her coach because she knew she would rush to her side when she started labour. If her mother was on a date, would she drop everything and come to Jane's side. She hadn't when Jane was in the hospital. How was she going to tell Sarah how adamant her mother was about her not being in the delivery room?

CHAPTER 9

The next day brought two surprises. The first was that the living room had changed back to black and white. The second surprise came when they got to class. They were each handed a robot baby to take care of for a week. The girls had been learning how to diaper, burp, feed and bathe dolls. Jane had even had a chance to hold a real baby for the first time in her life. She had not realized how wiggly they were until then. Now she had to take care of a robot baby for a week.

It wasn't long before Jane was struggling with exhaustion. The robot baby woke up every four hours to be fed. Jane was still feeding the neighbour's cat while the lady was visiting her daughter for a month in Arizona. She was also walking two small dogs twice a day, and weeding Mrs. Thurston's garden twice a week. She had to schedule everything so her mother wouldn't find out about the jobs. She was proud of the fact that she had saved one hundred and fifteen dollars for the baby.

One morning, she was feeding the baby a bottle with one hand and trying to eat a slice of toast with the other. She gave a big yawn. "You look exhausted," her mother said as she poured herself a coffee.

"This baby eats every four hours and by the time I fed it, changed it, burp it and put it back to sleep. I only get maybe two hours of sleep at a time."

Her mother laughed. "I know that is what taking care of a baby is like. It is worse for a single mother because she has no one to give the baby to for a few hours to get some sleep. You must be ready to tend to the baby twenty-four hours a day every day. That is why I keep telling you to give the baby up. You are only fifteen. How are you going to get an education or a job and take care of a child? What will you do when you are up all night because the baby is teething, and you have a final exam the next morning and you need to study? It is a tough job to do on your own."

Jane yawned and began burping the robot baby. "I think I will put us both down for a nap," Jane said as she stood up.

"Oh, by the way, I have some friends coming over tonight," her mother said with a big grin on her face.

Just what I need, Jane thought as she crawled back into bed. When she woke up with the baby crying, she got up to find the house silent. Her mother had gone out to get supplies for the party. So, she feed the baby and went back to bed.

That night, the house was rocking with singing and dancing to a karaoke machine that was blaring in the living room. Alcohol was flowing like water. The robot baby was fussy and crying and the only thing, Jane wanted was peace and quiet.

She was experiencing one of her migraine headaches. They had started a month before and she was having one every few days. Dr. O'Brien had done some tests but had not found the cause for them yet. Her head was pounding with every beat of the music, her stomach was queasy, and she had been having bouts of diarrhea. Lights bothered her eyes so she was sitting in the dark rocking the baby trying to get it to go to sleep so she could lie down.

When the urge to go to the washroom hit her, she hurried out of the room with the baby in one arm and her crutch in the other. She dodged around couples who were talking in the hall way as she made her way to the washroom. When she came out, a drunken man grabbed her arm insisting that she dance with him.

"Leave me alone. I can't dance. I have a cast," she cried as she tried to break free from his grasp. The drunk gave another pull and Jane lost her balance. The robot baby toppled to the floor as Jane instinctively grabbed for something to break her fall. Her fingers found material and she grabbed on tight. Her momentum sent her to the ground ripping the man's shirt as she went. She hit the ground with a thud. The jar of the fall went through her body. Dr. O'Brien's words flashed across her mind that any bump or fall may send her into labour. Was her baby old enough now to survive? Would she go into labour? She slowly got up. When she saw the robot baby with a crack in its head, she burst out crying. What if she had been carrying her baby in her arms? It would be dead. She picked up the robot and her crutch then hobbled back to her bedroom slamming the door behind her. She jammed the barrel bolt into place and lay down on her bed.

Her mother began pounding at the door telling her to open it. Jane screamed back, "You endangered my baby with your partying. I don't want to talk to you." Eventually her mother gave up and went back to the party which did not stop till four in the morning.

Jane lay on her bed in the fetal position holding her angel doll and the robot baby in her arms. She was afraid to move encase it would start her labour. She kept praying over and over that her baby would be all right. The hours ticked by as she wondered if she had the baby now could her mother force her to give it up. She was still a minor. She realized that she really wanted to keep the baby but how when so many strange things were happening to her.

The next morning, she called Sarah early and told her to meet her in front of Tim Horton's. Sarah was shocked at Jane's appearance. She hadn't seen Jane for a few days. She had had the flu and had been in bed for four days. Jane had dark circles around her eyes and her hair looked brittle and dull. She even looked like she had lost weight.

"Are you all right?"

"I have a headache and I am exhausted. Mother had one of her parties last night. It lasted until four in the morning when the police finally showed up. They threatened to charge everyone there with disturbing the peace if they didn't go home immediately."
"You look terrible." Sarah said with concern in her voice.

"I fell last night. So, I spent most of the night afraid that I would go into labour."

"Should you see Dr. O'Brien?

"I don't have an appointment with him, but I feel achy and sore all over especially on my left side where I have another big bruise. I have had a headache for two days now which seems to be getting worse. Also, my robot baby is broken." Jane said as she showed Sarah the robot's head. I don't know how I am going to explain this to the teacher. I wonder how much it will cost to repair it."

"Tell her what happened and have her send your mother the bill."

Jane cracked a smile at that. "Let's go in and get a coffee. Did you bring the forms like I asked to get my birth certificate and social insurance card?"

"Yes, but I thought you were going to ask your mother about your birth certificate?"

"I did and she swears she has not seen it since my father died. She has searched for it and has not found it."

"That is strange where would he have put it? Also, why would she wants it?"

"I don't know but I have to get out of that house as soon as I can and to do that I need my birth certificate."

"Did your mother give you the money to get it?"

"No, I have been doing odd jobs around the neighbourhood."

"When did you have time with the baby? I just struggled to get enough sleep and get the things done to keep the baby happy." Sarah exclaimed.

"Let's get the coffee and then we will talk," Jane said as she paid for the items and led Sarah to a secluded table by the washroom. "I have to tell you some things that may end our friendship," Jane said as she put her trembling hand on Sarah's.

"Jane, what is going on?"

"Remember when I told you I heard ringing when there was no sound."

"Yea, but that is nothing to worry about."

"Listen, Sarah. I hear the phone ringing and when I answer it no one is there. Mother doesn't hear it at all, but I do clearly, and the sound is coming from the phone not inside my head. Things that I have used are found in odd places when I am sure I put them where they belong. My room being the wrong color in my memories from what the photos show. I have even walked into the living room and found the color of the rug and the paintings have changed. I am hearing noises all the time like something being dragged over the floor yet when I check no one is in the house with me. I am afraid that I have brain damage and might hurt my baby or yours if I move in with you."

"When did this start," asked Sarah as she wrinkled her forehead in thought.

"It began the first day that I went home."

"You are normal around me. I don't like this something is not right."

"Oh, and when I told mother that I wanted you for my delivery coach she went ballistic."

"Do you think she will try to force you to give up your baby?"

"You know that she harps at me all the time about me being too young to raise a baby."

"We need to get a place as soon as we can," Sarah said with determination.

Relief spread through Jane as she realized that Sarah still wanted her as a friend and a roommate. "Thanks for believing in me," Jane said as she wiped tears from her eyes with her hand.

"We are going to get our place together somehow." Sarah said as she handed Jane a napkin to wipe her tears with. "Oh, I have some news for you."

"What," Jane said as she wiped her nose.

"Bill is in jail. He seriously injured a cop when they tried to arrest him. The police told me that he will be going to jail for a long while. It is like a huge weight has been lifted off my shoulders. Also, my brother called me and said I could see my mother. It has been so long since I saw her, I wonder if she will remember me."

"That is great news, Sarah."

"Now, I think we have a couple of things to do," said as Sarah stood up. "We have your forms to mail and then we are going to the hospital for you to get checked out."

"I don't have an appointment with Dr. O'Brien."

"When he hears you fell, he will examine you. Let's get going."

At the post office, Jane filled the forms out and popped the money order into the envelope. Jane finally felt she had accomplished something to keep her baby. She had told Sarah about the things that happened, and she took the first step to getting Social Assistance.

As they were walking to the hospital, Sarah got the impression there was a man following them. He never varied the distance behind them even when Sarah stopped several times to look in shop windows to see if he would pass them. She didn't say anything to Jane because she didn't want to worry her. Sarah was worried for Jane's welfare but why? Jane didn't have money or power. Why would anyone want to hurt her? This went on for a few blocks until they got near the hospital and the man went down a side street.

Sarah wondered if the man hadn't really been following them after all. Was it just her imagination? She couldn't shake her feeling that something was wrong. When Dr. O'Brien heard about the fall, he examined Jane immediately. He didn't like the looks of her but again he didn't find anything out of the ordinary.

Jane showed the doctor the robot baby. This angered him because he knew how much the dolls cost but he liked Sarah's suggestion of sending the bill to Jane's mother. He took the two dolls and said he would return them to their teacher with an explanation.

When the girls left the hospital, they did not notice that the same man was following them. He had changed his jacket and taken off his hat.

CHAPTER 10

The month before, Jane had received a subpoena to testify at Mark's court case. Today was the dreaded day. She didn't know how she would react when she saw him. She was still having nightmares which woke her up at night in a cold sweat. Yet deep down, he was her baby's father and he had protected her on the street. She wished she didn't have to go but her mother explained that she had no choice in the matter.

Jane crawled out of her bed feeling like she had not slept a wink. She tried to eat but nothing stayed down. Her mother told her to dress in her good clothes but when she went to put her best blouse on it wouldn't stretch over her enlarged bust line. She decided she would put a sweater on since it would stretch. She went to her sweater drawer and grabbed a sweater out. As she pulled it out of the drawer, a book fell out of it. That is odd, she thought as she picked up the book and read the title. It was a book her father had told her to read just before he died. She wondered how it got there. She didn't remember putting it there. She threw the book on her desk and continued her search for something to wear.

Finally, she came into the kitchen wearing a light blue sweater that clung to every curve but at least it covered her belly. Her slacks were baggy sweat pants that fit over her cast and belly.

"You can't wear that!" her mother exclaimed.

"The only things that fit me are my baggy sweat pants and old tee shirts."

"Why didn't you tell me? What time do we have to be at the courthouse?"

Jane went to the refrigerator where the subpoena hung by two magnets, "ten o'clock."

"It is eight o'clock now and I have not even started to get ready, so, we don't have time to go shopping. Come with me."

Jane followed her into her room. Her mother opened her closet doors and began searching around in it. Jane was shocked at the amount of clothes in it. She never remembered her mother having all these clothes when her father was alive.

Her mother grabbed a blouse off a hanger and tossed it to Jane saying, "Put that on."

"This is your good blouse. The one father gave you just before he died," Jane said as she began to struggle to get out of the tight sweater. "You can have it. I have plenty of others to wear."

Jane had loved this blouse when her father had showed it to her. It was red silk with gathering along the bust line. It had roses embroidered on the wide collar. She put it on wondering how her mother could so casually give away the last gift her dying husband had given her.

Her mother then handed her a black pair of dress pants with elastic in the waist and flared legs. The legs were to long but otherwise they fit her perfectly. Her mother pinned the legs up. Jane spotted herself in the mirror and realized that this was the first time since her father's death that she was dressed up. It made her feel good until she remembered why she was dressed up then she became nervous and scared at what would happen at the court house.

Her nervousness increased when they were late leaving the house because her mother couldn't decide on what to wear. They kept hitting red lights on the way and almost got in an accident. This just made the situation worse.

Her mother led her to the court room, and they sat down outside it. When Jane's name was called, Jane wished she could run in the opposite direction. A man in uniform escorted her into the court room and told her to walk to the front of the room while he stayed guarding the doors. She wondered as she timidly walked forward if he had read her mind and was guarding the doors so she could not escape.

As she walked by Mark, he made a fist and hit his other hand with it.

This made Jane more upset. Was that a threat that he would beat her up again? The thought of another beating from him terrified her. She realized then that he didn't care for anyone but himself. He had tried to kill her and her baby in a fit of rage.

She was told to raise her right hand and put her left hand on the Bible as she was sworn in. She then sat down in the witness box as the prosecutor approached her.

"Jane, did you live on the streets?"

"Yes."

"You lived with Mark."

"Yes, he protected me on the streets."

"Do you remember the beating you received on June fifteenth?"

"A bit about it," Jane hadn't told anyone that her memory of the beating had almost totally returned. That was what filled her nightmares almost every night.

"Did Mark always drink?"

"Yes," Jane said as she wrung her hands together.

"How did he act when he was not drinking?"

"He was harder to get along with."

"Had he every hurt you before?"

"No"

"Had he ever beaten anyone else up?"

"Yes, Jake."

"Why?"

"Jake told me that Mark had taken his booze several times and drank all of it himself which had angered Jake. He had finally stood up to Mark and Mark beat him severely." Jane said, Mark had told me that he had beat Jake up because he had shared his booze with Jake often and this time Jake refused to share it with Mark which angered him, and he beat Jake up. I didn't know who to believe since they both love their booze."

"Did Mark have alcohol that morning?"

"Yes, we had fought that morning because he took all the money we had to get the bottle of rum."

"Where did you go after the fight?"

"I went to the garage two blocks away like I do every morning to clean up in their bathroom. Tillie had seen me throwing up in the alley a week before and told me I was pregnant. I took a bit of money from my panhandling money each day and bought a pregnancy test. I took it that morning and I was positive. I felt hungry all the time and I was afraid the baby wasn't getting all the food it needed. So, I was determined to tell Mark that morning.

"Where you scared to tell him, you were pregnant?"

"I thought he would be happy about the baby. He had told me that he wanted children and a house someday."

"That isn't what Tillie testified to earlier today."

"I was wrong. He lied to me. The first thing he said to me when I told him I was pregnant was that he was going to make sure I lost the baby and that is when he started hitting and kicking me." Jane spoke out as tears started rolling down her cheeks.

"How old are you?"

"In a few months, I will be sixteen."

"Did you know that Mark is twenty?"

"No, he told me he was seventeen."

"Who is the father of your baby?"

"Mark, he is the only man I have ever been with." Jane said as a murmur went through the court room.

"That is all the questions I have for you at this time," he said as he turned and walked back to his desk.

The defense lawyer stood up with a defeated look on his face, "I have no questions for this witness."

Jane left the stand wondering if Mark had ever loved her or had only used her for his needs. She felt hurt and betrayed by him, yet she had the baby which she felt was a gift from heaven.

She later learned that he went to jail but she never was told what he was charged with.

Chapter 11

The next morning, Jane's mother was nursing a huge hangover. She was on her third cup of coffee and had already taking several aspirins. She had promised to take Jane shopping for clothes today. Jane had already eaten breakfast and was sipping at the health drink her mother insisted she drink every morning. She didn't feel very well and would have rather curled up on her bed, but she felt if she didn't go shopping today her mother would never buy her any new clothes.

At first, they dragged their feet as they went store to store in the mall but eventually, they began to feel better and they began to enjoy themselves. They went to all the hip shops, Old Navy, the Gap, Winners, and other stores. They giggled at the strange outfits they saw some people wearing and loved the outfits that they saw others in. They tried on mounds of clothes and each bought a few outfits. They even bought some baby items. At lunch, they ate at the crowded food court and shared a piece of rich chocolate cake afterwards. For the first time in a long time, Jane felt like she had gotten her mother back. She felt happy.

That is until she got home. They were barely in the door and her mother was on the phone making dinner plans with someone. Jane was facing another night alone. She cooked a TV dinner and ate it in the kitchen when someone knocked on the back door but when she looked out the window, no one was there. She felt scared and lonely. She decided that she would read the book that she had found in her sweaters.

She was only a few pages into the book when she found the word "Anchor" underlined. That had been her father's nickname for her. He never did tell her why he called her that. She had asked him several times and he would reply, "You are the anchor in my life." As she continued reading, she found other words that were underlined. She wondered why but the book was interesting, so she ignored the underlined words and just kept reading.

After an evening of several phone calls with no one on the line, three doorbell ringing incidents, and someone tapping on her bedroom window, and reading until three in the morning, Jane had slept in. She woke up to the sound of her mother talking on the phone in her bedroom next door.

"Did you get everything I need… good, I will get them on my way to work." "Mom, I am awake," Jane called as she stretched and climbed out of bed. She headed to the shower.

When she came into the kitchen, her mother was drinking her coffee at the table. "Your drink is ready on the counter over there. I have to work till three."

"Ok," Jane as she sipped at the protein drink. She made a face as it seemed more bitter than usual.

After her mother left, Jane went out to get the mail. There was a letter addressed to her. Who would be writing to her, she wondered as she started to open it? It turned out it was a letter from the government. It informed her that no one by the name of Helen Evans had given birth to a child on her birthday in this city. They would need more information to get her a birth certificate. What did this mean? Were her parents not married when she was born? Was she born elsewhere? Was she adopted? Was this why her mother wouldn't give her the birth certificate?

Jane called Sarah and read her the letter. She was just as confused as Jane about how they were going to get the information out of her mother. Jane also told Sarah about the underlined words in the book her father wanted her to read.

"Maybe it is a message or something. He was dying when he told you to read it and it could have been him that put it among your clothes so you would find it and read it. Go through the book finding the words and see if it is a message," Sarah said excitedly, "This is like a mystery we have to solve."

"It will take a while, but I will call you when I am done. Talk to you later."

Jane spent the afternoon going through the book page by page. When she heard her mother come home, Jane quickly closed the book and stuffed it under her mattress with the note pad she had written on.

Her mother had brought home Kentucky Fried Chicken. They sat down and started eating.

"Mom, do you remember when we went to Disneyland?

"Sure, I do, it was the only time your father took us anywhere. We only went there because you asked to go there," her mother said grudgingly. "I always wanted to travel but your father never wanted to."

"Disneyland is in the States. Do you need a birth certificate to? go there?"

"You did at that time. Now you need a passport. What brought this on," her mother asked as she looked at Jane with a frown on her face.

"At class today, they told us when the baby was born, they would give us forms to get the baby's birth certificate. That everyone needed one of them. I never saw mine. Where is it?"

"I have not seen it since your father died. I don't know what he did with it. I wish I did," her mother sounded a bit angry.

Why was her mother angry that she couldn't find Jane's birth certificate? Jane wondered. She decided to search the house, garage, and work shop. She started the minute her mother left on her date. She started with the living room. There were few places to hid things in this room. The only place that took time to search was the bookcase. She took out one book at a time and shook it hoping that her birth certificate would fall out. She then put them back in the same order so her mother would not notice that anything had been moved. She then moved on to the dining room. The chairs and table were bought after her father had died so this room was done. The kitchen had been redone also. If his father had hidden anything there it was long gone. Jane was just opening the door to her mother's room when her mother came home.

Jane quickly shut the door and headed to the living room. "That date sure did not last long, "Jane said as she glanced at the clock on the wall.
"The guy had a bad headache so we decided that we would go to the movies another night."

"Well, I was just going to watch some television," said Jane. "Are you going to join me?"

"No, I think I am going to go to bed early for a change," her mother said as she headed toward her bedroom.

Jane really did not want to watch television, but she turned it on and sat watching it until she thought her mother had gone to sleep. She then went in her room and locked herself in. She grabbed the book and her notebook from under her mattress and finished going through the book. She read over the words several times then laid on her bed wondering what her father meant.

Chapter 12

Jane was scheduled to see Dr. O'Brien. She got up early to bathe and went to her room to put on one of her new outfits. When she put the outfit on the blouse was three sizes too large and the pants were too small. What is going on she wondered. I just got this outfit and it fit me perfectly in the store. She changed into her other outfit and the same problem occurred only this time the pants were huge, and the blouse was too tight. Jane changed into her baggy pants and yellow tee shirt and went to the kitchen.

"Why are you not wearing one of your new outfits? Don't you see the doctor today?" her mother said as she stirred sugar into her coffee.

"Well…err…there must have been a mix up at the store. The outfits don't fit me."

"What! You must be wrong," her mother said as she left the room and came back with one of the outfits. Put that on."

Jane stripped off the tee shirt and put her new blouse on and it fit her perfectly. The pants also fit.

"What is the matter with you? You are putting things in wrong places. You are hearing things. Now you are saying things don't fit you when they do. When you see the doctor this morning, you better tell him. If you don't, I will," her mother threatened. "I have to get to work," she said as she headed to her bedroom to get ready.

When Jane was ready to leave, she went to the front closet to get her shoe. She couldn't find either shoe. They must be there, Jane thought. She had been trained all her life that when you come in the house your shoes go in the front closet. Fifteen minutes later, she found them both under her bed. Why were both shoes under her bed? She had only been using one since she returned home because of her cast.

Her mother's words haunted her all the way to the hospital. How could she tell the doctor? He may think she would be an unfit mother and she really wanted to keep her baby. She sat stewing about it until the doctor entered the room.

Dr. O'Brien noticed that Jane looked even thinner than the last time he had seen her. She had dark circles under her eyes, and she looked very worried about something.

"How are you feeling?" he asked.

"I have been sick at my stomach every day almost and the headaches are almost continuous."

"Morning sickness is part of being pregnant. Usually it occurs earlier in the pregnancy but occasionally it waits to the last stages. I will try you on a different medication for your stomach maybe that is what is causing some of your discomfort. Are you eating well?

"I am trying to. Mother is making me a protein drink every morning with fresh fruit. It is supposed to contain all the vitamins and minerals I need. Unfortunately, it seems to taste bitter to me, but I drink it to keep her happy."

"It sounds like you mother is coming around to the idea of having a granddaughter in the house."

"Not really, she wants the baby to be health so someone will adopt it fast. She is continually making comments on how a baby will affect my life."

"The chose to keep your baby is yours. I will stand by your decision. Here is the prescription and more vitamins to take. I want you to take two a day. Also, your ankle is swollen see," as he pressed his thumb into the area above the ankle bone on her good leg. When he removed his thumb, "See the dent stays where I pushed that means your body is holding water. So be careful of the salt you eat.

Jane did not tell the doctor that she was craving French fries and potato chips.

"When do you get the cast off?"

"I have an appointment with the doctor at eleven thirty today, I can't wait? It is so itchy it drives me crazy at times. I just hope he decides that it can be taken off."

"Are you getting enough sleep?"

"I…I try to get eight hours if I can, but the headaches make it hard to get to sleep." Jane did not tell the doctor about her father's note that kept her up most of the night trying to figure out what it meant.

"I am going to send you for another ultra sound and some other tests," the doctor said as he handed her the lab order. "I don't like your weight gain and your appearance."

"Ur…ok," Jane said as she decided not to tell Dr. O'Brien about the things happening at home.

Jane went to the basement of the hospital to the lab and then where the ultra sound was done. When she saw the image of the baby on the screen, she was surprised to see how developed her baby was. She was elated when the nurse gave her a picture of the baby. Every day that passed made the baby more and more real to her. How was she going to keep her baby? She had to figure out what was going on. What bothered her was that the strange things only occurred at her house. When she was with other people, nothing strange happened. Why?

Jane got her wish and the cast was taken off. She couldn't wait to get home and call Sarah. She told her about what happened that morning with the outfit and that her cast was gone.

"That is odd," Sarah said.

"What is strange is the message my father left me," said Jane.

"It was a message in that book?"

"Yes, but I can't figure it out."

"What does it say?"

"It says:

> *Anchor,*
> *Hidden is a treasure trove,*
> *Hidden behind a tiny cove*
> *Information it contains*
> *Something that will sustain*
> *Bringing out many lies*
> *And different family ties*
> *Tell no one about this*
> *I seal this with a kiss*
> *Love Dad*

"What do you think it means?" Jane said as she picked up a glass of milk and took a sip.

"It sounds like your father hid something for only you to find."

"He must have been the one who put that book in my sweaters."

"Can you think of where this cove is?"

"I have never been to the beach with my family. Dad and mother didn't swim. Only with my friends who go to the public beach and there is no cove there.

"There has to be another meaning for cove."

"Do you have a dictionary? I haven't got one here," said Jane. "I looked for one before I called you.

"Meet me at the library in an hour and bring the message."

"Ok," Jane said as she put the message into her purse.

She hurried to the kitchen and made herself a sandwich which she ate quickly. She grabbed her purse and left the house.

When Jane reached the library, she spotted Sarah sitting on a bench just inside the front door. They went to the second floor and passed the row of computers. They found the dictionary on a pedestal at the end of a long row of book shelves. They turned the pages of the dictionary to the right place and scanned the page until they found the word cove. It did have another meaning. A curved moulding at the juncture of a wall and a ceiling. They found a quiet corner of the library and poured over the message trying to figure out what it meant. They made a copy of it so Sarah could have one. Two hours later, they left and went their separate ways still not any closer to the meaning of the message.

Jane did not expect her mother at home until very later. At least that is what the note said on the kitchen table. So, she decided to finish searching the house, she searched the laundry room, the bathroom, and her mother's room but didn't find a thing. There were only two places left in the house to search. She figured that she could search her room any time. So, she decided to head for the attic. She knew her father often stored things up there. As a child she loved to explore up there.

Jane went to the hall and pulled down the attic ladder. She carefully climbed the stairs. The smell of stale air and old musty things surrounded her as she turned on the flashlight she had brought from the kitchen. She found the switch that turned on the bare bulb that hung from the ceiling. It illuminated the boxes, furniture, and chests that were covered in cobwebs with big fat spiders on them. She cringed as she brushed away the cobwebs. She hated spiders but she had to figure out where this cove was. She felt that her father left her the message because it was important. She found the furniture that her father had built piled up in one corner. That made her smile as she searched each piece looking for a secret compartment in it. She didn't find anything. She turned her attention onto a box of old toys and baby furniture which filled another corner. She then began looking into the old trunks and the other items in the attic. About two hours later, she found an old wooden box. It was beautifully carved with two doves kissing on the top. When she opened it, she discovered a picture of her father with a different woman holding a baby. She was sure the baby was her but who was the woman. She had almost finished the search when she heard her mother enter the house. Jane quickly put the picture and wood box into an old chest that she had just opened and shut the lid.

Jane heard her mother stumbling into the house cursing as she kicked off her shoes and tried to hang up her sweater which kept falling off the hanger. Jane knew her mother was drunk and hoped she wouldn't raise her mother's suspicions of what she was looking for in the attic.

"Whas tis?" her mother said as she came into the hall and found the attic stairs down.

"It is only me," Jane said as she walked over to the hole in the attic floor.

"Whas ya doing?" slurred her mother as she tried to climb the ladder.

Jane looked down at her mother. "I just thought there might be something of mine up here I could give the baby. I found this stuffed animal," Jane said as she grabbed a dirty discoloured teddy bear which was missing an eye and one ear that was sitting near her.

"Can's giff baby ith," as she missed a step and fell.
"Are you all right?" Jane called down to her.

"Tired…bed," as her mother got up and staggered into her room.
Jane made a quick search of the chest then climbed down taking
with her the wooden box and photo. She hid them in her room and
then returned the ladder to its place in the hall ceiling.

Chapter 13

Jane curled up on her bed surrounded by all the family albums after her mother left the house. She went page by page. She carefully examined each picture in hopes of figuring out who the lady was in the picture from the attic. There was not a single picture of the lady. Who could she be? Jane wondered. She loved her father and her. You could see it in the way she was looking at them.

Jane noticed that there were very few pictures of her under three years old. She found that odd because she was an only child and most parents have hundreds of pictures of their first baby. This bothered her. Could there be more pictures of her somewhere else? She had not found anything in the house. She knew her mother would be suspicious if she found Jane in her father's workshop but that was the last place to look. Jane had to come up with an excuse to be in the workshop for long periods of time.

Jane put the albums back in the living room book shelves and got ready to go to work at Mrs. Thurston's house. An hour later, she had almost finished weeding the long flower bed that stretched the length of the front porch of the large brick house. Mrs. Thurston came out on the porch and looked over the railing at Jane.

"Jane after you have finished, will you come into the house."

"Sure, but I am a bit dirty," answered Jane as she pulled the last three weeds out of the garden. She then slowly got to her feet and stretched.

"Throw those weeds in the compost heap," Mrs. Thurston said as she pointed at the wheelbarrow full of weeds. "Wash your hands at the outside tap and wipe them on this towel," she said as she put the towel over the railing.

Jane did as she was told and went to the front door and knocked as she kicked off her muddy shoes and brushed off her clothes to get as much dirt as possible off her.

"Come in, my dear," Mrs. Thurston called from the kitchen. "I am getting us something cold to drink. Have a seat in the living room."

The scent of fresh baked cookies surrounded Jane as she stepped into the entrance hall. The living room was arranged with soft cushiony couches and older wood tables that shone and smelt faintly of lemon oil. She wished this was the type of furniture her mother liked. The place felt homey and welcoming. Jane slowly walked around the room examining all the pictures that sat on the tables and shelves. There were dozens and dozens of pictures of different children.

Mrs. Thurston entered carrying a tray of lemonade and homemade cookies and put them down on the coffee table.

"You must come from a very large family."

"Actually, these are all my children."

"Yours! How could you possibly have all these children?" Jane exclaimed.

"I could not have any children of my own, so my husband and I became foster parents. We filled the house up and when one left, another came in. In all, I helped raise over fifty children."

"Fifty! I am nervous about trying to raise one."

"What a child wants is love and discipline?"

"Discipline, they know you love them if you take the time to set rules for them and make sure they are disciplined if they break the rules. But enough on my beliefs, will you go to that closet and take out the two garbage bags that are in there."

Jane struggled to pull the bags toward Mrs. Thurston. "What is in them? They weigh a ton," exclaimed Jane.

"Just some things my women's club collected for you."

"For me," Jane said with a surprised look on her face.

"Open the first bag."

Jane sat down on a foot stool beside the first bag and began pulling out item after item. Tears began rolling down her face as she pulled out baby clothes, blankets, bottles, diapers, and other items that she would need for her baby.

"I won't have to buy hardly anything for my baby. How can I ever thank you and your friends for all this."

"You can thank us by being a good mother," said Mrs. Thurston with a big smile. She was happy that she could bring such joy to Jane who always seemed sad to her.

Jane gave Mrs. Thurston a big hug. She asked Mrs. Thurston if she could come to her for advice on child rearing.

"Sure, but what will your mother say about that."

"My mother doesn't even want her granddaughter. She wants me to give her up because I am so young. I want to keep the baby, but I haven't figured everything out yet. I will have to get on Social Assistance and my girlfriend Sarah and I are planning to move in together and help each other. Sarah is a little older than me and has babysat before. I never was around other children other than at school. In fact, I never held a real baby until I took a class at the hospital a few weeks ago. So, if we have a problem we can't solve with our babies, can we call you? We will need an expert like you to help."

"I never thought of myself as an expert, but I guess I have seen about anything a child can get into. You and your friend are welcome to call me or visit whenever you want to," Mrs. Thurston said with a chuckle. She filled the glasses with lemonade and handed one to Jane. "Have a cookie. They are best when they are still warm."

"Hmmm…they are delicious. Would you give me the recipe?" Jane asked as she reached for a second one.

"Of course, but the secret is to serve lemon cookies with lemonade. It makes them taste better," Mrs. Thurston winked.

They sat and talked for about an hour about the challenges that Jane would face as a single parent.

"Oh my," Jane said when the grandmother clock began to chime. "I have to get home and cook dinner. Can I borrow your wheelbarrow to carry all these things home?

"Sure," Mrs. Thurston said as she slowly got to her feet.

"I can't thank you and your friends enough for all this," Jane said as tears welled up in her eyes as she gave Mrs. Thurston a hug.

"We are just glad we could help you."

Jane hurried home and stuffed the bags in her closet. She then returned the wheelbarrow to Mrs. Thurston's before her mother got home. She couldn't wait to tell Sarah about the baby items, but Sarah was at the doctors, so she had to wait. Jane had just started the chicken roasting in the oven when Chuck knocked on the back door. He told Jane he came to collect his money for mowing the lawn. Jane looked around the house, but her mother had not laid any money out for him. He decided that he was going to wait for her mother. She offered him a drink of iced tea and he sat at the kitchen table while she peeled potatoes and made a salad for dinner. At first, Chuck talked about the weather and other neutral subjects. Then out of the blue he asked her, "How do you intend to support the baby?"

"Err…I haven't figured that out yet."

"Do you have a boyfriend to help you or money stashed somewhere?"

Jane felt very uncomfortable and wondered. Why was he interested in what she intended to do? What did he want?

Just then her mother opened the back door. Her arms were full of groceries. Jane went to help her. She grabbed a bag of groceries from her mother just as her mother noticed Chuck sitting at the kitchen table.

"What are you doing here?" she angrily barked at Chuck.

"I came to get my money."

"Jane put the groceries away," she said as she put the other bag of groceries and her purse on the counter. "You come with me," her mother said as she led Chuck out of the house.

Jane began to put things away, but she kept glancing out the window at her mother and Chuck who seemed to be arguing about something. She wondered what had upset her mother so. She decided that she wouldn't tell her mother about the baby items until she was in a better mood.

Her mother barely talked to her that evening. They silently watched television until nine o'clock when Jane excused herself saying she was going to read. Instead she went into her room and cleaned out one of her drawers. She was just starting to put the baby clothes into the drawer when she heard her mother go out.

Chapter 14

The next morning, Jane called Sarah and they decided to go to Tim Horton's for coffee. She put on one of her new outfits and it was huge on her. The sleeves covered her hands and the pant legs needed to be hemmed up by one inch. Jane knew this was not the outfit that she wore a few days before. Then it had fit her perfectly. Why were these things happening? She changed into another outfit that fit and hurried out the door.

When Jane arrived, she stood around looking for Sarah. She didn't see her until Sarah waved at her. Jane had not recognized her because Sarah's hair was now dark brown and cut shorter. She was sitting at the far table near the washrooms.

"You look so different. Why did you change your hair colour and hairstyle?" Jane asked as she sat down at the table.

"I went back to my natural colour because I won't have the money to colour my hair after the baby is born. Bill was the one who wanted me to be a blonde. I also figured if I was going to start a new life with my baby, I would need a new look. So, what is up?" asked Sarah.

" A few things have happened. I looked through the family albums and I didn't find this lady's picture anywhere." Jane said as she shoved the picture toward Sarah. "I also noticed there were very few pictures of me as a baby."

"That is a bit odd but maybe your parents could not afford a camera when you were young."

"That is possible. I had something great happen."

"What?" Sarah said as she picked up her donut and took a bite.

Jane told her about all the things that Mrs. Thurston had given her.

"You are lucky. I hardly have anything for my baby," said Sarah.

"I was thinking about that. We will be able to share things when we are living together that will help both of us."

"Thanks, that will help," Sarah said as she pushed open the door. "I have been thinking of the clue your father gave you. Do you have any moulding near the ceiling in your house?"

"There is a bit in the kitchen, but I have already checked it out and it is solid and not moving."

"I wonder what your father meant."

"I wish I knew," Jane said.

They left Tim Horton's and walked to the bus stop. They had planned to go to the community college to get information about getting their high school equivalency degrees. When they sat down on the bench, Jane swung the large purse she was carrying off her shoulder and put it on the ground beside her. She then leaned back against the back of the bench so that the baby who was kicking up a storm had more room.

Sarah sat talking about their plans for an apartment together. She was thinking of going to yard sales and flea markets to get things they would need. All the while she talked, Jane sat quietly because she was not feeling very well again. She was still having bouts of nausea daily. She had also noticed this morning that her hair seemed to be getting thinner. In one way, she couldn't wait to give birth to her baby. Maybe then she would feel better.

The bus pulled up. Jane reached down to get her purse. It was gone. The girls looked all around but it was nowhere to be seen.

"I had my bag here, didn't I?" Jane asked as she rubbed her forehead. A headache was starting again.

"Yes, I saw you put it down beside you when we sat down."

Jane sat back down and put her head in her hands. The bag had the picture of that lady in it, the copy of the message, the book and the money she had earned that week in it. What was she going to do?

"You should call the police."

"Not yet," Jane said. "Will you go back to Tim's with me?"

"Sure, but why?"

"At home when something is missing, if I retrace my steps the thing appears again in a totally different spot than I had put it."

"But I saw you take you bag off your shoulder here and put it down here," said Sarah "Why go back there?" as they began walking back to the coffee shop.

"Just humor me before we report it to the police," Jane said feeling agitated and nervous. Was this what was happening at home? Was someone else moving things on her? But a lot of the time, she was home alone. She had to be the one putting things in odd places.

Sure enough, the bag sat on the floor beside the chair that she had been sitting in twenty minutes before. Jane grabbed it up and checked to make sure that everything was still in it.

"I don't understand. How did the bag get here?" Sarah said as they left the building.

"Come with me," Jane said as she led Sarah to a park bench across the street. "You knew that strange things were happening around my house."

"Yes, you told me," Sarah said wondering were this was leading.

"At first, I thought I had brain damage from the beating until you pointed out that I was normal when we are out together. After that I tried to figure out why these things were happening just around the house. I even wondered if we had a ghost or something that was haunting me because I could not come up with a logical solution until last night.

"What happened last night," Sarah asked.

"I am beginning to think it has something to do with my father's note. He mentions a treasure." Jane said as she fished the note out of her bag. "I realized that last night when Chuck started asking me a question?"

"What questions?"

"Whether I had money stashed somewhere to support the baby?

"That is an odd question," Sarah said as she rubbed her chin.

"Whoever is doing it fouled up today?" Jane said.

"What do you mean?"

"Everything that happened was always at home. Today, the person moved my bag while I was in a public place to make me think I was getting worse, but he failed."

"How did he fail? We still don't know who is doing this."

"He failed because you saw me put my bag down at the bus stop and I didn't move from there until the bag disappeared. I didn't move it. You are my proof that I am not going crazy or have brain damage."

"Why would he move it if I was with you and could prove you didn't do it?"

"He didn't realize that you were still with me," Jane said excitedly.

"We didn't leave each other's side," Sarah said with a confused look on her face.

"Remember when we left Tim's, we stopped at the side of the building so you could put your ball cap on which covered your hair now that it is short and your sunglasses on. With your dark hair hidden and those glasses on, the person may not have recognized you and thought I was sitting at the bus stop alone."

"But we were talking to each other?"

"No, you were talking, and I was listening. I was nauseated again, and I was just sitting quietly. He may have thought you were talking to the lady who was sitting on the other side of you."

"I don't get it. Why make you think you were crazy? You have no money or power."

"I don't know yet, but the person failed. I now must figure out who it is and why the person is doing this? Will you help me?" asked Jane as she placed her hand on Sarah's.

"Of course, I will. You are my friend and you are not crazy."

"Thanks for that vote of confidence," Jane said with a smile.

"Do you think it is your mother? She wants you to give your baby up and everything is happening in her home," Sarah said with a serious look on her face.

"It can't be her. That day she was there at the table when the phone rang. She didn't hear it. Lots of times I am alone in the house when something happens like the noises. I have checked the house and I am totally alone in it. I have even called her work to see if she is there when the furniture changed around, and the colours changed. She was at work because I called the stores number and she answered the phone.so how could she be doing things. It just can't be her."

"Does she want to get rid of your baby so bad she is trying to force you to give it up?" asked Sarah.

"When it comes to the baby, she is just worried that I won't get an education or meet someone. Who would want me right now anyways? I look like a barrel with legs and arms. I vomit all the time and average a bad headache three or four times a week."

"I thought the new medicine the doctor gave you was helping you."

"It is a bit, but I still feel terrible a good portion of the time.

"Have you told Dr. O'Brien? Is that normal?" Sarah was becoming more and more worried about her friend.

Oh," Jane said as she snapped her fingers, "I forgot to tell you. I found the photographer who took the picture of the lady, my father and me. His name was on the back of the photo when I took it out of the black holder it was in. Will you come with me to his shop?"

"Sure when?"

"Let's go now. It is on the way to the college. I want to see if he knows who the woman is."

"That picture was taken years ago, how would he remember that?"

"I know it is a slim chance, but I have to try. I think she has something to do with all that is happening."

"Why do you say that?" questioned Sarah.

"It is just a feeling I have. She seems somehow important to me but I don't remember her that is what has me confused."

"Let's get going then. Another bus should be coming soon," said Sarah as they started walking back to the bus stop.

Ten minutes later, they were standing in front of a brick building with a large window supporting a sign that said, Hanson's Photo Studio. They opened the door and walked in.

A man was working at a long table near the back of a long narrow room. Once he saw them, he came to the counter which separated them from his work area. The walls were lined with all kinds of pictures from portraits to beautiful scenery. A chemical smell seemed to permeate everything. The hum of a large printer spitting out pictures filled the room.

"Can I help you?" the dark-haired man asked.

"I was wondering if you could possibly tell me who paid for this picture and who is in it?" as Jane held up the photo to the gentleman to look at."

"Boy, this is an old one, but you may be in luck. This number on the back tells me that the picture was taken in February of 1999. My father set up that filing system years ago and I learned it when I began working here during summer vacations. You may be in luck. When I took over the business a few years ago I never took the time to clean out his files. The man went over to a row of ancient wood filing cabinets and began looking for one marked with the right code on it. It didn't take him long to find the correct drawer and pull out an old musty folder. Returning to where the girls stood leaning on the counter, he said, "This photo was paid for by Mrs. Evans."

"Mrs. Helen Evans," questioned Jane.

"No, it was Mrs. Pauline Evans."

"Thank you …err…thank you for your help," stammered Jane.

She didn't know anyone by that name. Who could this lady be?

"Do we owe you anything," added Sarah.

"No, glad I could help. My father was a pack rat and kept everything. Would you like the other pictures that were taken at the same time?" asked the photographer.

"I would love them," said Jane hoping they may lead her to an answer of who this lady was.

"There are three of them, handing Jane the old file.
Sarah peeked over Jane's shoulder as she opened the file and looked at the picture of a small baby who looked like Jane.

"That picture is in the family album at home." The next picture was of the lady. "I don't remember this lady, but I feel like I should know her," Jane said as they left the building.

"Wait, let's go back in," Sarah said as she turned back to the entrance of the building.

"Why?"

"You told me that you thought your room was yellow before you left home and now it is pink and the photos prove it."

"Yes," Jane said as she wondered what Sarah was thinking.

"Let's ask him how difficult it would be to change a photo."

The photographer was just hanging up the phone when they

returned. "Sir, can you tell us how easy it is to alter pictures and change colours? Thinks like that."

"With the new computer systems, they have out, you can change backgrounds, colours, write on them, and do almost anything to them. All you have to do is scan them into a computer that has the program in it," said the photographer.

The girls thanked him again and left the studio.

"What was that all about," asked Jane.

"What if your mother changed all the photos in your album of your bedroom?"

"Why would she go to all that trouble? All she had to say was that she had my room repainted. I don't understand what is going on." Jane replied.

"Come with me to the newspaper building. We may be able to find out who Mrs. Pauline Evans is," said Sarah.

"How do we do that?"

"You will see," said Sarah with a smile.

CHAPTER 15

The girls got off the bus and walked towards the modern glass edifice that housed the newspaper. As they approached, the glass doors slide open inviting them into a large brightly lit reception room. A large sculpture of the world with the word News across it filled one corner of the room. A long sleek desk occupied the opposite wall where a lady sat talking on the phone. In the background, they heard the clamour of phones ringing, people talking, and the hum of large machines.

"Excuse me," Sarah said when the lady hung up the phone. "Where do we go to look up old newspaper articles?"

"Go to the elevator around the corner. Take it to the basement and turn right when you get off. Mrs. Copeland will be there to assist you."

They followed the instructions which lead them to a small carpeted room which was divided into small work areas. Computers set on all the desks but one where a machine sat that Jane had never seen before.

"Can I help you?" asked a white-haired lady in a mint green suit who smelled like lavender?

"We would like to look at your old newspapers," said Sarah.

"We don't keep old newspapers. Everything is either on the computer now or a microfiche machine."

"What is a microfiche?" asked Jane.

"It is an older method of storing information and uses that machine over there," Mrs. Copeland said as she pointed at the machine that Jane had wondered about. "What year did you want to look at?"

The girls looked at each other and shrugged their shoulders as they had no idea where to start.

Finally, Jane stammered, "My birthdate is November 25, 1998.

"That year is on microfiche," said Mrs. Copeland as she went to get everything they would need and then showed them how to work the machine.

The girls leaned forward as they started staring at the screen as they scanned page by page looking for anything that linked to Jane's family. After half an hour, the girls were rubbing their eyes as they discussed how to speed up the search.

"We may be searching for months before we find a mention of my family in the newspaper," Jane said discouragingly.

"I have been thinking," said Sarah. "This lady has your father's last name, so she is either a female relative or his wife. Did your father ever mention having a sister?"

"No, he was an only child."

"Then let us assume she was his wife and your mother," said Sarah.

"That doesn't help us much," Jane said as she rubbed her stomach where the baby was kicking her.

"Not necessarily," Sarah said, "What do mothers and fathers do when they have a new baby?"

"They tell the family and friends," Jane said.

"How do they tell them?"

"Phone, announcements, oh… I get it birth announcements in the paper."

"Yes, I just thought of that a few minutes ago. If we just skip to the birth announcements instead of reading the whole paper it will cut our time in half at least," Sarah said as she moved the machine to read the next day's birth announcements. They found the announcement in the November twenty-seventh newspaper.

A turmoil of different emotions flooded into Jane as she read it. It said that Henry and Pauline Evans were happy to announce the birth of their daughter Jane Rebecca Evans. Jane sat there trying to get around the fact that the mother she knew was really her step mother. Then sadness hit her when she realized that she didn't remember one thing about her real mother. Questions started popping into her mind. Where was her real mother? Why was she not in Jane's life? Jane felt tears begin to roll down her face. She tried to wipe them away before Sarah saw them.

She wasn't quick enough. Sarah saw the tears and gave Jane a big hug.

"Why did she leave us?" questioned Jane."

"There could be a whole lot of reasons," Sarah said as she fished some tissues out of her purse and gave them to Jane. "She could have been an alcoholic or drug user. She could be mental unstable or even be dead. You may never find out what happened."

"There has to be a way to find out," Jane said as she wiped her eyes. She then blew her nose loudly.

"Do you remember anything about her?"

"No," Jane said as she began to weep some more.

"She may have abused you, so your father took you away from her."

"No, she loved us just look at the picture." Jane grabbed her bag and began rummaging in it until she found the picture and pulled it out. She put it in front of Sarah. "See her look, she loved us."

"Well, you were not kidnapped or taken from her because you would not be living in the same city under your real name. Maybe she was mentally ill or died."

"The paper has obituaries. Will you help me look?" Jane asked Sarah.

"Sure, I will help. You are my friend."

"Thank, I need to know."

"If she died, when do you think it happened? Do you remember anything odd when you were little?"

"I remember the only time I saw my father cry."

"What happened?"

"He came home, and his eyes were all red and puffy. He sounded all stuffed up. He gave me an angel dressed in a long golden gown with white feather wings. He told me that I would always have an angel watching over me. He hugged me so tight that I could hardly breathe and began to cry. Its kind of scared me and I began to cry with him, but I really didn't know why I was crying. You know that doll did seem to comfort me when I was growing up. Whenever I am upset, I curl up on my bed with it until I felt better. I still have it. It sits on my dresser at home."

"How old were you when he gave you the angel?"

"Two maybe three," Jane said as she dabbed at her eyes again.

"I wonder if he was crying because your mother had just passed away."

"Let us start looking at the obituaries after I turned two."

It was a long tiring search as they went day by day through the obituaries. Minutes turned into an hour. The babies protested the cramped position their mothers put them in as they leaned forward staring at the machine's screen.

Finally, on February 14, 2001 they found the obituary of Mrs. Pauline Evans. It stated that she died of liver cancer after a two-year struggle. She left behind her husband and her daughter. She was an heiress to a large shoe manufacturing company.

"Jane, your mother was wealthy, do you think this is the treasure trove your father mentioned in his message."

"I wonder. My father worked for a shoe company but if he owned it why did he live so modestly. He never had a new car, or fancy home. Yet, I always had everything I ever wanted. I can remember my mother…. I mean stepmother asking for things and my father telling her they would have to save up for it. She used to get so angry and they would fight sometimes over money. If he owned the company, my stepmother wouldn't have to work."

"A company doesn't disappear out of a family unless they sell it, or it goes bankrupt. This company is still in business today, so it didn't go bankrupt. If he sold it, there is a large sum of money somewhere that he tried to tell you about in that message."

"My mother…I mean stepmother, would have gotten the money. That must have been the money to remodel the house."

"She hasn't spent the kind of money that the sale of a large company would generate."

"Should I ask my moth…. I mean stepmother about the money?"

"I don't think so. With all the strange things happening around you and your father's warning, I think you better keep quiet about her being your stepmother and about the money. Remember to play dumb." Sarah warned.

The girls packed up their belongings and headed for the elevator. As they exited, Sarah bumped into Chuck who looked like he was going to get on the elevator. Instead he gave the girls a startled look and dashed out of the building.

"That was odd. I thought he was going to get on the elevator," remarked Sarah.

"Chuck, definitely acted like he saw a ghost," said Jane as they walked out of the building.

"Chuck, the guy you said your mother was angry at!" Sarah stopped and looked around trying to figure out where the man had gone to. She didn't like the nagging uneasiness that filled her. "Jane, promise me you won't let it slip what we have discovered. Something is going on and I am afraid for your safety."

"Don't worry. I will be fine," Jane said before she left Sarah and headed home.

CHAPTER 16

Jane was tired when she got home, and she went to sleep watching television as she waited for her mother to come home with another takeout dinner. Jane wondered sometimes why her mother spent all that money on the new kitchen when it was hardly used. When her mother arrived home, she began questioning Jane on what the girls had done all day. Jane remembering Sarah's warning. She lied saying they had window shopped most of the day.

"Mrs. Holt told me she saw you go into the newspaper building today," her mother said.

"Oh…yah we went there also." Jane hadn't seen Mrs. Holt at the newspaper office just Chuck. "Sarah was trying to find a place to live. She must leave the Women's Shelter soon. She also was looking at things for sale and maybe a job." Jane blurted out trying to cover up the real reason for them being at the newspaper.

"I am worried about you. You are isolating yourself from all your old friends. The only person you see is this Sarah. You hardly know anything about her. I don't think she is who you should be hanging around with. She is older than you for one thing. Connie's mother told me that you saw Connie at the store a while back and you refused her invitation to go to a party. What is going on with you?"

"Nothing, I like Sarah. She understands what I am going through. She understands that I want to keep my baby. Not like you. All you do is preach to me about all the reasons to give my baby up."

"Do you really think you are fit to raise a baby? You are fifteen with very little education. How would you support a baby? How often do you put things in the wrong place or forget to do things I ask you to do? I can see you forgetting where you put the baby or forgetting to feed her."

"You will see. I am going to be a good mother to my baby," Jane cried out as she burst into tears and ran into her bedroom. She slammed the door and snapped the bolt into place.

She tried to ignore her mother who called through the door, "This type of behaviour only proves that you are acting strangely, and you definitely look terrible. I am worried about you. There isn't a day that goes by that you don't do something strange. How often have I seen you pick up the phone and it hasn't rung? I ask you to do things and they are never done."

"You haven't asked me to do anything."

"See what I mean. You don't remember me asking you to putout the garbage this morning."

"You didn't ask me to put the garbage out," Jane called back through the door.

"Yes, I did last night, and you didn't do it, did you. This is what I mean. You are not fit to raise a baby."

"I am going to be a good mother, I am, I am," Jane cried out as she sank to the floor against her door and began to sob.

"Think about what I said," her mother called.

Fifteen minutes later, Jane got up off the floor. She grabbed her angel doll and curled up on the bed. Was she acting strange like her mother said? She lay there pondering her mother's words. Why didn't a counsellor notice if she was acting strange? Those counsellors were trained and dealt with beaten women every day. If something was wrong with her, they would have spotted it. Was she responsible for the strange things happening at the house? She was alone most of the time when they happen, but she hadn't moved her purse, but it had moved. Sarah knows she hadn't moved it. If she wasn't doing them who was? Her mother couldn't be doing them, yet she was the one who wanted Jane to give up her baby. Why didn't her mother want her to keep her baby?

Jane got up and stood in front of her floor length mirror. She did look terrible like her mother had said. Dr. O'Brien had run tests but had not found the reason yet. Her hair had begun to be frizzy and unruly. It was also falling out. She had dark circles around her eyes, and she felt so tired all the time. Her vomiting had not stopped even with the medicine the doctor had given her. She wondered if she should go back to see Dr. O'Brien before her next appointment. Maybe she had liver cancer like her real mother and would never get to raise her baby like her mother. This thought terrified her. What would happen to her baby if she died? She was positive that her stepmother would not raise her daughter.

When it came to her old friends, she had not called them, and they had made no effort to contact her. She had only seen them that one day, but it showed her that she didn't fit in with them any longer. They were carefree going to dances, playing sports, and going to the beach. She was pregnant. Who would want to dance with a beach ball with legs, she thought as she looked at her plump round figure in the mirror? She would not look cute in a bikini with all her stretch marks showing. She wasn't even interested in boys right now. A boy had gotten her into this mess.

Why couldn't her mother understand that she had changed in the last year? Sarah was experiencing the same things and working for the same goal to keep her baby as Jane was. She felt closer to Sarah than she had ever felt with any of her old friends. Was there money somewhere for her like her father's note suggested? Was someone trying to make her think she was crazy so they could get the money like Sarah had suggested. Her mind went around and around in circles until nature called and she had to head to the washroom. She quietly opened the door and headed down the hall. She heard her mother talking on the phone in the living room. Jane stopped to listen.

"We only have three weeks left…we need other people to see it… we need to think of something before it happens …see you tomorrow." Her mother hung up the phone and lit a cigarette and went out of the front step to smoke it.

Jane went to the washroom and returned to her bedroom wondering what was in three weeks. She went to the calendar on her desk. She then realized that her sixteenth birthday was in three weeks. Was that why her mother had been talking to Connie's mother? Was her mother planning a birthday party for her with all her old friends? What did other people have to see? All her old friends would know by now that she was expecting. Before what happens? The only things that was going to happen was that she would give birth soon. Maybe it was to show her friends the scares on her face. Did her mother think that the scares were keeping her from seeing her old friends? They did make her feel self-conscious, but the girls had already seen them.

This was so out of character for her mother. Jane had never had a birthday party. She had only had a cake and a special dinner at home with her father and mother. Was it because it was her sixteenth birthday? Jane lay on her bed wondering about what she had heard until she fell asleep.

CHAPTER 17

Jane woke up the next morning lying on her bed in the clothes she had worn the day before. At first, she couldn't remember why she had not changed and gotten into bed properly. Then she remembered the argument with her mother and the strange phone call.

When she went to the kitchen, she found a note from her mother saying she was golfing and would be gone most of the day. She was eating breakfast when she glanced at the calendar on the wall and realized she had a doctor's appointment. Her appointment was in an hour and she hadn't got dressed yet. She rushed around getting ready and headed out the door. She was ten minutes late for her appointment, but the doctor's nurse squeezed her in between the doctor's next two patients. Dr. O'Brien was worried about Jane. She looked worse than the last time he saw her. He still could find no reason for what she was suffering with.

It was eleven o'clock when she got home. She had barely opened the door when the phone started ringing. She hurried to answer it. It was Sarah calling.

"Do you want to go shopping today for items for my new apartment?" Sarah asked.

"New apartment, when did this happen?"

"Last night. I had put in my name for geared to income housing when I first got here. I was put at the top of the list since I can't stay at the shelter much longer and I am expecting a baby. The counsellor told me that they had a two-bedroom apartment for me. I can move in immediately if I want to."

"Where is it at?"

"Do you know the apartment building beside the West Side High School?"

"Sure, I do. That isn't far from here." Jane felt comforted by the fact that she wouldn't be that far away from Sarah's apartment.

I was told it has a refrigerator and a stove, but I must come up with the rest of the furniture and household items. I have two hundred and twenty-five dollars to spend so I am on a very tight budget. So, are you ready to help me shop?"

"I sure am."

"Do you have any ideas where to get some good bargains? I was thinking flea markets and yard sales."

"They are good, but you may not find everything you need right away. When I lived on the streets, I shopped at the Salvation Army Thrift Shop. They have furniture, household items and clothes cheap."

"My main problem will be getting the stuff to the apartment."

"They have a truck. I have seen it. They may deliver the items for you. You may have to pay a fee."

"I need so much. I need a kitchen table, chairs, sofa, tables, lamps, television, bed, dressers and a crib to buy."

"You won't have enough money for all that. You must start with the basics. After that everything else is a luxury."

"I have to buy food for one week out of this money also. I guess you are right. I must have just the basics. So, when do you think you can get to the Thrift Shop," Sarah said excitedly?

"I have to eat and change into older clothes."

"Jane, are you just getting up? Are you feeling all right?"

"I just got back from the doctor's, but I had a rough night, I will tell you about it when I see you," Jane said. "I have to change into older clothes because if you are dressed poorly you can get better deals there.

"Ok," Sarah said. "I guess I better change also into older clothes. See you in an hour."

Jane hurried and got changed and left the house.

When Jane arrived at the Thrift Shop, Sarah came up behind her and covered her eyes, "Guess who?"

"I think it is the bargain hunter. Are you ready to find some? deals?" Jane giggled.

"You bet. Let's get started." Sarah said as they walked into the red brick building that looked like a converted warehouse. The front of the building was full of clothes. There was every size and colour of item a person could imagine.

Jane led Sarah to the back of the building where the household items were situated. They saw a large assortment of beds, couches, and chairs. As they moved around, they looked at price tags and did the math in their heads. Sarah knew she also had to get groceries and cleaning supplies with the money. "Jane, if I buy anything, I won't have money for food."

"They had a food bank here also. That will help with your budget. Let's start with the basics, like I said. What is the price of that mattress only?"

"The price tag says twenty-five dollars."

Jane walked over to the clerk who was sitting near the cash register filling out some form. "Sir, do you charge for delivery of large items?"

"We charge five dollars."

"Thanks," Jane said as she returned to where Sarah was standing admiring a blue loveseat with a lot of fluffy cushions.

"Sarah, it will cost you thirty dollars to get the mattress. If you get it, you can use it as a couch during the day and a bed at night with some pillows. You need blankets, towels and cooking items. Then next month you can buy something else."

Sarah sighed as she turned away from the loveseat she had been envisioned in her apartment. "You are right. I can't have everything at once. I just wished I could buy that loveseat. It is beautiful."

"If you bought that you couldn't sleep on it. It isn't long enough. Do you want to sleep on a hard floor for a month?"

"You are right. I have to be practical." Sarah took a last look at the loveseat and then turned her attention to mattresses.

"That single mattress could be put on wooden crates to be used as a sofa during the day and a bed at night. The crates can be used for storage also."

"I need baby things also,"

"For a crib you can use a large laundry basket with a blanket folded in the bottom at first."

"When I first got pregnant, I dreamed of Bill helping me fix up the baby's room with cute furniture and lots of animals and letters over the walls. Now I can't even afford a crib for my baby," Sarah said sadly.

"No, but your little girl will have the most important thing, a mother who loves her."

After Sarah paid for the mattress and arranged delivery of it for later that day, they shopped for pillows, a blanket, a set of sheets, two place settings, utensils, two small pots and a frying pan. They found two towels, a shower curtain, a bath mat and a wash cloth all in matching colour. They then went to the food bank and Sarah got enough food to last her for a week. She even had some money left.

They had just walked out of the door loaded down with boxes and bags. They had planned to go to the bus stop on the next corner, when Sarah spotted Chuck across the street. He had turned away just as they came out of the door like he was trying to hide his face from them. Was he following them? Jane had told Sarah about her argument with her mother. Was that how Jane's mother knew about them being at the newspaper? Sarah wondered? She didn't like it and didn't want him to know where she would be living.

"I don't think we can carry all this stuff to the bus stop," Sarah said as she pretended to struggle with the packages she was carrying. She put her packages down on the ground and hailed a passing taxi. The taxi pulled over and Sarah told Jane to get in the front seat as she loaded the items they had into the back seat. She then slides in beside them and gave the driver her new address.

"I thought you were watching what you spent. A taxi isn't cheap," Jane said.

"Well, I guess I will just have to eat a lot of mac and cheese until my cheque comes in next week," Sarah said trying to cover up her uneasy feeling about Chuck. "We could never have gotten all of these things to the apartment," Sarah lied as she glanced over her shoulder. Chuck was trying to hail a taxi. Sarah just hoped that he would not be able to follow them.

The taxi pulled up in front of the apartment building, Sarah had the money to pay him ready. She hurriedly grabbed her packages from the back seat and rushed to unlock the front door of the building. Sarah and Jane carried the packages into the building. Sarah looked around to see if she spotted Chuck anywhere. She didn't see him which eased her mind a bit as she checked the door to make sure it was locked behind them. The girls headed for the elevator to get to Sarah's new apartment on the second floor.

As Jane entered the apartment, Sarah looked around to see if anyone had seen them enter it. No one was around which made her feel a little better. She closed the door and checked to make sure it had locked behind them.

"Welcome to my new digs," Sarah said trying to calm down so Jane wouldn't realize what just happened.

Jane entered a small hall that divided into two entrances. One was to the living room which was a long slender room with a picture window at one end. The other entrance led to the kitchen. The stove and refrigerator were on one wall and the cabinets and sink were on the other. The walls were beige, and the cabinets were brown. At the end of this area was a place to put a small kitchen table and chairs. Beside that was another entrance that opened back into the living room to the right.

Jane continued exploring to find that all the rooms were painted beige. On the other side of the living room was a hall that led to the two bedrooms and a tiny compact bathroom. None of the rooms were large but it was perfect for Sarah and the baby. Jane felt a touch of jealousy because Sarah was making a home for her baby and she couldn't even get identification papers to start the process.

"I wish I was making some headway at getting a place for me and my baby," Jane said.

"You have a place with me. but I think we need to figure out what is going on around you first," Sarah said. "In the meantime, let's get started at turning this place into a home."

The girls unpacked the bags. They washed down the cabinets and put the washed kitchen items away. They discussed the most convenient arrangement for the dishes, can goods, and pots as they did it. They put the shower curtain up and hung the towels in the bathroom. The last touch was to put the bath mat on the floor. They had just finished up when the buzzer rang on the intercom. The men had arrived with the mattress. They came up and put in in the living room as she instructed.

"I can't believe this is all mine. I feel like I am home," Sarah said as she closed the door behind the men who had delivered her mattress. The girls put sheets on it and the blanket. Sarah threw the pillows on the mattress and told Jane to sit down and rest. Sarah made tea for them and sat down beside Jane. "Has anything else happened at home?" Sarah asked. She wanted to ask Jane about Chuck without arousing Jane's curiosity.

"I think my mother is planning a sixteenth birthday party for me."

"What makes you think that?"

"I heard her on the phone with someone."

"That will be fun. What do you want for your birthday?"

"My birth certificate so I can keep my baby."

"We will find it and get to the bottom of what is going on," Sarah said with determination. "Do you think Chuck will be at your party?"

"I doubt it. Mom was so angry at him the other day. I don't know if he will even cut our lawn again. Oh, did I tell you I thought of how to search my father's workshop?"

"How?"

"My crib and high chair were in the attic when I searched up there. I want to fix it up for my baby. Mom will most likely protest because she is still pushing for me to give the baby up. I will just have to be forceful about fixing them."

"That is a good idea. You will need those items for your baby and you know how to fix them."

"It will allow me to be in his workshop for hours without her being curious of what I am doing as long as I make some progress on the furniture that she will notice if she comes in to see what I am doing. Oh, look at the time," Jane said as she glanced at her watch, "I have to be home by five to make dinner tonight."

"I have no phone here yet, but I have to go back to the shelter for tonight, to get my things. I will call you in the morning."

"Ok, I will talk to you in the morning," Jane said as they went down the stairs and out the door.

Sarah kept an eye out for Chuck as they walked to the corner where they had to part ways. "Be careful. I just have an uneasy feeling."

"I will be fine. Don't worry." Jane said as she turned down her street. "Talk to you tomorrow."

Sarah stood and watched Jane walk down the block. Why was Chuck's appearance today at the Salvation Army bothering her so much, she finally turned and walked to the shelter?

CHAPTER 18

That night at dinner, Jane broached the subject of the baby furniture in the attic. "Mom, I want to fix up the crib and the high chair in the attic for my baby."

"What do you want those old things for?"

"I will need them for my baby."

"You are not going to give up, are you? How are you going to support a baby? Don't expect me to support you and the baby? I am already working more hours than I want to just to keep this place going."

"Don't worry I won't ask you for money to help with your granddaughter," Jane said sarcastically.

"I am just trying to think of your welfare. Anyway, a pregnant woman is not supposed to be around paint."

"Don't worry. Father has a great air filter mask he used when he sanded and painted because of his allergies. Wearing it, I won't even get a whiff of paint."

"You will need a new mattress for it and the crib is against regulation now because the bars are too far apart."

"Then I will take it apart and add more bars to it. It will actually make it easier to sand when it is apart, I can put the bars on the lathe and sand it that way," Jane said sidestepping all of her mother's objections. She went out in the hall and pulled down the attic ladder.

She carefully climbed the ladder and began dragging the crib pieces and the high chair to the opening in the floor. She then handed them down to her mother who reluctantly helped her daughter get them out of the attic.

Jane put the items by the back door so she could take them out to the workshop in the morning. Shortly after that her mother left saying she was going to the movies. Jane went into her room and took out the sheet with her father's message. Jane sat wondering what her father was trying to tell her. She got up and wandered from room to room looking for this cove that her father had mentioned. She knew he liked secret compartments. Where could it be?

She closely examined the painting in the dining room of a sailboat skimming across the water of a bay. The paper was not ripped on the back of the oil painting. Could something be hidden behind that paper? She got a knife and carefully slit it and peeked behind the paper. She didn't find anything.

In the kitchen, she got up on a chair and checked out the moulding around the kitchen cabinets again. She found nothing. She finally gave up in frustration and went to bed. She didn't sleep. Her father's note and the idea that someone was trying to convince her that she was crazy floated round and round in her head. Why? Were they after the treasure her father talks about in the note? Where would her father have hidden it?

The next morning, she dragged herself out of bed. She drank the protein drink that her mother had left in the fridge for her. As she got cleaned up and dressed, she decided that she would get the furniture to the workshop and start working on it. When she got the furniture to the door of the workshop, she discovered that it was locked. Where would the key be? After looking in all the kitchen drawers, she found the key stuffed in the corner of her mother's bedside table. She knew she would be yelled at searching her mother's room, but she took the key to the workshop.

When she opened the workshop door, the hinges creaked as the door opened. Cobwebs hung from the ceiling and she heard the scurry of little feet as she entered the room and flicked on the lights. She realized that no one had entered this room since her father had died months ago. She moved around the room touching things and wondering if it was the last thing her father had touched. Finally, she decided that she had to get something done. She would have to clean before she could get started on the furniture. She grabbed a broom and started brushing away cobwebs. Dust coated everything. She got some old rags from the house and a bucket of water and began wiping off the tools and work benches.

By one o'clock, she was exhausted. She finally sat down in her father's big wood chair he had made for himself and looked around the room. She wondered if this is where she would find the treasure her father talked about. He had been extremely organized. He had taught her that everything had its place and once you were done using it. You put it back in its place so it would be there when you needed it again.

Jane began looking around trying to remember if anything seemed out of place. She got up and slowly moved around the room. She soon discovered the router was not in its place. A birdhouse sat there instead. She picked it up and began examining it. She lifted the roof flap, but nothing was inside of it. She turned it over and noticed that the bottom seemed thicker than usual. She started feeling every corner with her fingers to see if she could find a hidden latch or spring.

"Jane."

The birdhouse crashed to the floor as Jane jumped. Her heart was pounding as she turned to find her mother standing there.

"Mother, you startled me. I was just thinking that this birdhouse was the last thing father was working on before he passed away?"

"How did you get in here?"

"I...ah...searched for the key. I know that I shouldn't have searched your room, but Dad always kept the key to the workshop on him. So, I thought that if you had found it in his belongings after he died you would have just thrown it in a drawer somewhere. I am sorry but I wanted to get started on the baby items."

"We both miss your father a lot, but you do not have the right to go through my things," her mother said angrily.

"I am sorry, but...," Jane said as she picked up the birdhouse off the floor and a piece of paper floated to the floor. Her mother quickly reached down and grabbed the paper before Jane could. "What does remember the cove mean?" asked her mother as she
read the note.

"Father must have made a note to remind himself to put cove, a type of trim on the birdhouse," Jane tried to say it casually trying to hide the fact that her mother might be holding a clue to the treasure. Jane noticed that there was writing on the back of the note. Her mother shoved the note into her pocket and said, "Sarah called. I told her that you were out because I didn't realize you were in here until I came out to get into the car to go to work. We are going to have an early supper because I have a big date tonight."

"Do you want me to have it ready for when you get home?" asked Jane.

"No, I will just bring pizza home."

"I just want to fix these things for my baby."

"I haven't got time to get into this now. I will see you tonight." Her mother turned and left the workshop.

Jane watched her as she walked to the garage. She took the paper out of her pocket and tossed it into the garbage can before she climbed into her car and drove away.

Jane waited until her mother was down the block before she rushed to the garbage can and searched it for the slip of paper her mother had thrown away. When she found it, she went back to the workshop and read the back of the note. It said:

Remember the work.

She sat down in her father's chair. She pondered this for a long time, but nothing came to her. She finally decided to straighten the workshop then go in and call Sarah.

When she picked the birdhouse up to put it back where her father had left it, she noticed a slight opening at one corner. It seemed like something was in there preventing the drawer to slide open. She took a screwdriver and pried the piece off the birdhouse. Inside was a key that was wedged in so the drawer couldn't slide open all the way. She took needle nose pliers and pulled the key free. She then replaced the piece she had pried off so if anyone looked at the birdhouse, they would not notice the secret compartment.

She looked around the room trying to figure out what the key opened. She searched the drawers and cupboards but there were no locks. She looked under the work benches and in the rafters. Nothing needed a key. She finally shoved the key into her pocket with the note and closed the workshop. She went into the house and called Sarah.

"Hi, Sarah, you called earlier."

"Yes, I stayed at the shelter last night and I was going to go to the apartment earlier today but when you didn't call, I got worried. I was just going to go to your place and see if you were all right. You didn't tell me you were going somewhere this morning."

"I was out in the workshop. I found the key this morning in my mother's night table. I had to clean the shop before I could start working on the baby items. It gave me a chance to explore his workshop. I found a note and a key. The note says: *Remember the cove* and on the other side, *remember the work*."

"What does that mean?"

"I haven't figured that out yet. Mother is going out tonight so I am going to search the house and see if I can find something that the key works in. There was nothing in the workshop that required a key."

"Do you want me to come over now and help you search?"

"No, mother said she was going to be home early, and she saw the note. I pretended that it was just a memo Dad must have made for himself. I hope she believed me."

"How did she see the note?"

"Dad had hidden the note and the key in a birdhouse he had made. I dropped it when mother startled me. The note fell out and she took it and threw it in the garbage. I fished it out and read it. I think I am going to lie down in my room and just try to remember what my father and I did before he died. I don't feel that well anyway and I feel exhausted."

"Jane, are you all right? You seem to be tired a lot and you still are having morning sickness."

"I will be fine. I am just going to lie down and think about what my father is trying to tell me."

"I will be at the apartment this afternoon. There is a telephone on the corner. I will call you later."

Jane went to her room and lied down. She began thinking about the projects her dad had worked on before he passed away. She loved woodworking like he did. She remembered them laughing and talking for hours while they worked on some project. They had made and repaired all kinds of things for their friends and neighbours. She soon drifted off to sleep.

She woke up with a start when a loud slamming noise echoed through the house. What was that? Who was in the house with her? She heard a sound like something heavy being dragged over the floor. She climbed out of her bed and went to the door. She cautiously opened the door a sliver and peeked out. No one was moving in the hall. She grabbed her tennis racket and tiptoed down the hall. The sound seemed to be coming from the living room. She got to the doorway and peeked around it. No one was there. The noise had stopped. What was going on? What had made the noise? It had been loud enough to wake her, yet no one was here. Had she imagined it?

She slumped into a chair as the fear she had felt drained from her. Yet confusion still filled her thoughts. She was still in the chair holding her tennis racket when her mother came home ten minutes later.

"Why are you sitting there with a tennis racket?"

"Oh, I dropped a pen behind the couch. I tried to reach it with the racket. The baby didn't like it and I started having a sharp pain in my stomach, so I sat down," Jane lied.

"Are you all right? You are not starting into labor?"

"No, I don't think so," Jane said. "I think I just twisted my body the wrong way and I had a cramp."

"Put the pizza on the table for me while I get my shoes off. Are you hungry?"

"Yes." Jane said as she realized that she had not eaten since breakfast. Maybe that was why she felt so bad, she wondered as she went into the kitchen.

Over dinner, Jane listen to her mother preach to her about all the reasons she should give her baby up. Jane insisted that she was going to keep her baby. This upset her mother who left the house in a huff. Jane however was beginning to have doubts that she would be able to keep her baby. She still had no way of supporting a baby. She had to find the treasure mentioned in her father's note. She felt exhausted and emotionally drained, but she had to keep searching.

Jane went room by room searching for something the key fit into but to no avail.

Two hours later, the phone rang. Jane answered it.

"Hi, Jane did you find anything?"

"No, Sarah."

"Did you think of what your father meant by the work you were to remember?"

"We made a bunch of things together. When he got sick, he took time off work and he spent most of it in his workshop making things for people. I helped him after school and on weekends."

"Did he make you anything special?"

"Yes, a jewellery box but there is no secret compartment or cove on it. I have gone over everything I can think of and nothing stands out."

"Think on it overnight. Maybe something will come to you. I am now officially moved to my apartment. I did what you said today and picked up some old crates. I also went to a garage sale and picked up a lamp and a clock for five dollars."

"Sounds like you have a cozy place ready for your baby. I just wished I could say the same."

"You will. You always have a home with me."

"Thanks Sarah, that makes me feel better."

"I will call you in the morning."

Jane had thought she was going to have a quiet night. That was until she had someone knock on her front door but when she got there no one was there. Then the phone began ringing with no one there. The lights flickered on and off and she heard the dragging noise again. She felt so nervous that she locked herself in her room with her tennis racket beside her on the bed. She kept wondering if she really was imagining all these things. She kept coming back to her purse being moved at the bus stop. She had a witness that she hadn't done that but that was only one time out of hundreds that she could explain. She finally fell asleep around midnight with no answers yet of what her father's clues meant.

Chapter 19

The next morning, she sat in the kitchen eating a bowl of cereal when her mother with a large smile on her face entered the room.

"I am going to have some ladies over tonight. We are going to play bridge. Can you make sure your room is clean?"

"Why do you want my room clean? They are not going to be in it."

"Don't give me a hard time. I just want your room clean. You can also help me clean the rest of the house since you want to be a smart mouth."

"I was going to go out and work on the baby items."

"You can do that while I am at the grocery store but when I get back I want you to help me straighten the house and make the food."

Her mother left to go shopping and Jane hurried to the workshop to get started. When she unlocked the door and flicked on the light, she was stunned. Tools where scattered everywhere and the benches were pulled out from the wall. Who could have done this, she wondered? The door had been locked and she had the key. Did her mother have a spare key to the shop? Why would she ransack it? She wondered if the person found what she was looking for. She began cleaning up when Sarah knocked on the door and entered the workshop.

"What happened here?" Sarah said as she looked around.

"I don't know. It was clean and tidy when I locked the door yesterday."
"Was something taken?"

"I don't think so. I think the person was searching for what we are looking for." Jane said as she started to pick up tools and put them where they belong. Sarah started helping her.

"Do you think someone knows about your father's message to you?"

"When my purse was taken, the note was in my purse. The person could have read it."

"I don't like this," Sarah said uneasily. "Jane do you think you should move to my place."

"I promised my mother that I would help her clean the house and prepare food for her card party tonight. Besides if I go to your place, I won't be able to search for the treasure."

"I just feel that you are in some kind of danger."

"I will be fine. Oh, that is mother coming in the driveway now," Jane said as she looked out the window, "I will be helping her all day and we have company tonight. She is playing bridge with some ladies."

"Don't tell her I am here," Sarah said as she hid behind the door.

Jane's mother stuck her head in the workshop and said "Can you help me with the groceries?"

"Sure, Mom, I will just lock up and be right there."

"Hurry up. We have lots to do," her mother said as she went back to her car to grab some bags and took them into the house.

"Jane don't tell your mother I am here. While you are both busy inside, I can search this place while I straighten up for you. When I am done, I will sneak out the gap in the fence at the back, so she doesn't see me. I will call you later if I find anything."

"OK," Jane said as her mother called her name again. "Coming mother," Jane called out as she shut the door of the workshop. Jane went to the car and grabbed an armful of groceries and headed for the house. She spent the rest of the day cleaning, preparing food, and setting up the card table in the living room.

When the women arrived, her mother made a point of introducing her to them. Jane began to feel uneasy when she realized that her mother had invited all her friend's mothers. Her mother use to call these ladies snobs and busy bodies. Why would her mother ask them to play cards when she disliked them? Jane excused herself when the ladies sat down to play cards.

She went to her room with a large plate of desserts. When she opened her bedroom door, she saw her baby clothes all tore and ripped in a pile on her bed. Her angel doll was lying on top with a knife sticking out of it. Red liquid dripped from it onto the paper it laid on. Large red letters jumped out at her saying:

This will be your baby soon.

Her plate dropped to the floor and shattered into pieces. Jane started to scream and ran into the living room. All the women stared at her as she babbled incoherently about her angel being stabbed, her baby clothes and her dead baby.

"Jane, stay here. I will go see. You are most likely imagining everything." Her mother hurried from the room. A few minutes later, she returned with the angel doll in perfect condition. "Jane, you are hallucinating again. Here is you doll and there are no baby clothes on your bed. If you don't believe me, come and see for yourself. They all followed her to her room and looked in. Everything was neat and tidy except the broken dish and food on the floor." "I did see it, I did," cried Jane.

"Honey, you need to be checked into a psyche ward and get help. I am sorry ladies, but I think I must attend to my daughter. I hope you understand," she said as she escorted the murmuring ladies to the front door.

She shut the door behind them and began to smile. "You played right into my hand," as she looked at Jane who was huddled in a chair hugging her angel doll and shaking.

"I did see it! I did!"

"Yes, you did see it thanks to Chuck's help," her mother said as Chuck stepped into the living room with a nasty look on his face. If you hadn't ran into your old girlfriend this wouldn't have been necessary. Their mothers, the nosey old bags, started asking questions. You see I can't let your baby live and I can't let you live otherwise I can't become the heir of your inheritance. Those ladies now think that you are hallucinating, and you need to be committed to a mental hospital. They didn't know that I faked your commitment papers to a hospital already and your father's lawyer has been paying me handsomely for your care ever since you ran away," her stepmother said with a smile on her face.

"Once you both are dead, I become your sole heir and the inheritance your father kept from me for all these years will be mine, I will be able to travel and live the way I always wanted to. In the meantime, you are confined to your room," she said as she grabbed Jane and shoved her toward her room. Jane tried resisting but Chuck grabbed her and carried her to her room where he shoved her into the room. She fell on the floor and watched as her door slammed shut. Jane heard the dead bolt slide into place. They had taken it off her door and put it on the other side of the door.

She rushed to the door and tried to open it, but the door was not budging. All she heard was them laughing and celebrating. She went to her window and tried to open it. It wouldn't open. She threw one of her trophies at it. The trophy bounced off it and she realized they had changed the glass in her window to plexi-glass. Jane didn't know what to do. She sat down on her bed in complete hopelessness. She had to figure a way out but how. Sarah was the only one who knew about the things going on. Would they hurt Sarah also? She began searching her room for anything she could use to pry the window open. She tried a metal ruler, but it bent. A hanger bent. She was now beginning to panic and cry. They were going to kill her. She had to get out for her baby's sake.

As the hours ticked by, the house grew quiet. How could the mother she had loved to do this to her? Jane thought about her father, his clues, and her baby. She had to get away.

Around midnight, she heard a tap on her window. She looked out and saw Sarah signalling her to be quiet. She showed Jane a hammer and began prying nails out that had been used to nail her window shut. Sarah soon had the window open and whispered, "Get the book, the notes, the key, and the picture and let us get out of here before they wake up."

Jane stuffed them into her bag and handed it out to Sarah. Sarah put the bag on the ground and got down on all fours. "Step down on my back." As Jane got her bulky figure out the window, she felt a sharp pain in her abdomen. "Oh…!"

"Are you all right? We have to get out of here," Sarah whispered as she got back on her feet.

"I just had a pain. I will be fine, but we can't leave yet. We need to get one more thing," whispered Jane. "I know where my father hid something for me."

"Where?"

"In the big birdhouse over there," Jane pointed to the old tree with a bird house hanging from it.

"What?"

"My father made the birdhouse a week before he died. He was so weak at the time that he had me help him. I remember now that he used the word cove when he put some trim on it. He showed me the secret compartment and jokingly told me it was a perfect place to hide things from my mother. She considers birds dirty animals and avoids them."

"Well, let's get it and get out of here before they realize you are gone?"

Jane hurried to the birdhouse and stood on her toes to reach the bottom of it. She ran her fingers along the bottom trim until she found the latch and tripped it. A six-inch drawer snapped open. In it was a tin box. Jane grabbed it and shut the compartment.

"We better hurry," whispered Sarah, when the neighbours upstairs light went on. "We have to get out of here and get you to safety."

She led Jane to a small gap in the back hedge that lead to the alley. She got on all fours and crawled through. Jane followed as Sarah led her down the alleys and people's yards until they got to her apartment building.

"We can hide out here until we can figure out what to do next."

Sarah said as she unlocked the apartment door and they hustled in locking it behind them. They both dropped to the mattress exhausted and emotionally spent.

"How did you know that I was locked in my room?" asked Jane.

"When I was about to leave the workshop, I saw Chuck open your back door with a key. This bothered me because when we were at the Thrift Shop, I saw him watching the entrance from across the street. When we came out, he tried to hide his face so we wouldn't notice him. He was also at the newspaper office. This made me suspicious of him, I couldn't come up with any reason for him having a key to your house unless he was helping your stepmother. So, I stayed in the workshop and watched. Chuck never came out and the ladies arrived. I snuck out of the workshop and hide behind the shrub under your living room window trying to hear all that was going on. No one mentioned Chuck being there which was odd. Then I heard you scream. I didn't know what to do. I almost was seen when the ladies left the house talking about you hallucinating about an angel and your baby. Then when I heard your mother laugh and say she was going to get rid of you and the baby. I didn't know what to do.

I heard Chuck and your mother celebrating and talking about what they would do with all the money they would get by having you and your baby out of the way. I snuck around the house to your window and peeked in and saw that you were safe for the moment. I saw the nails in the window, so I went to the workshop to find a hammer and wait until it got darker out and they fell asleep.

Jane reached into her pocket and pulled out a key. "I know where this fits now," she said as she pulled the metal box from her bag. She unlocked the box and opened it. Inside was her social insurance card, her birth certificate, a lock of hair, a business card and a letter.

Jane began to shake as she opened the letter and began to read it out loud.

March 15th

"Dear Anchor,
I am writing this because I suspect that I don't have long to live. You always asked me why I called you Anchor. It was because you anchored me to my true love, your real mother, Pauline. The mother you know is a step-mother. There is a picture of your real mother in the attic in a box with two doves carved on its cover.
We had only been married about a year when she gave birth to you. Unfortunately, it was not long after that she was diagnosed with liver cancer. My heart broke when she died, but she made me promise that I would take care of you the best I could.
Helen was the housekeeper at the time. She took care of you

and ran the house while Pauline was sick in the hospital. After Pauline's death, I depended on her more and more to help care for you and when you started calling her mother, I decided to marry her.

After we married, she started questioning me about Pauline's money and where was it. I told her that Pauline had sold the business and used the money to pay her huge medical bills. In truth, Pauline left everything to you with me and her lawyer in charge of the trust until you turned sixteen. You were then to start learning the business from the ground up under the guidance of me and her lawyer.

Unfortunately, her lawyer passed away and a new lawyer took over. I always had all communications sent to my office so Helen would never learn the truth. Her interest in your money bothered me. You loved her even though she never took any interest in any of your activities or accomplishments. So, I didn't divorce her for your sake.

The new lawyer didn't know about my suspicions about my wife and sent a letter to the house telling me that he was taking over as co-trustee. Helen opened the letter and read it before I got home from work.

I didn't learn about the letter until two months later when I went to the lawyer for our regular quarterly meeting. By then I was already feeling ill and my doctor could not figure out what was wrong with me.

I heard a phone conversation between her and someone and I now suspect that I have been poisoned. Take the lock of my hair to the lawyer on the business card and get it tested.

I would have told you the truth outright, but your mother had made me promise that you would not know of the money until your sixteenth birthday. She wanted you to have a normal childhood and not one with a silver spoon in your mouth like she did.

Love father"

"Dad died a few days later," Jane uttered as she stared at the date."

"That is why you mother is so upset about the baby."

"What do you mean, Sarah?"

"If something happened to you, your baby would be you closest living relative and inherit the money not your mother. So, she must get control of the money before there is any record of the baby being born. If you are in a mental institution or dead without a baby, she would then have complete control over the money."

"That is why she didn't want you as my delivery coach. You could testify that my baby existed, and she wouldn't get her hands on the money. It would be in trust for my baby."

"We are taking you to his lawyer in the morning and prove to him you are not crazy," said Sarah with determination. "Right now, we need rest."

The girls curled up on the mattress together and were soon asleep from emotional exhaustion.

CHAPTER 20

Jane exited the bathroom looking terrible.

"Jane, you have been sick all night. Do you think you have been? poisoned like your father?"

"Maybe, you know I have been feeling lousy for months. But how? We ate frozen foods or takeout food mainly."

"Your mother made you a protein drink every morning."

"Yes, so I got all the vitamins and minerals that the baby needed."

"Maybe it was to get rid of the baby instead."

"That would be murder."

"She already did that once with your father so why not again."

"I didn't think of that."

"I am taking you to Dr. O'Brien after we see the lawyer."

"I guess I should to be safe."

The girls arrived at the lawyer's office a few minutes before nine o'clock and waited for the doors to be opened.

A young man dressed in a grey pinstripe suit with a light blue shirt and grey tie approached the door and unlocked it. The girls followed him into the office.

"Have you got an appointment?"

116

"Err…no," Jane said as Sarah nudged her, "But I think Mr. Oliver will want to see me."

"What business does he have with you?" asked the lawyer.

"I am Jane Evans. My father was Henry Evans and my real mother was Pauline Evans. My father left me this letter and lock of hair."

The lawyer took the letter and read it and then stared at the lock of hair. He also looked at her birth certificate and social insurance number. "I am Mr. Oliver but I am a bit confused here. I was told that you were in a mental hospital and I have been giving Mrs. Helen Evans a monthly allowance for your care. She showed me the documents of your commitment.

Sarah stepped in. "I am Jane's friend and she has not been in a mental institution. It was a plot to get the money mentioned in the letter."

"That is a serious accusation."

"You have been giving Mrs. Evans money for Jane's care," Sarah blurted out.

"Yes"

"It was not used for Jane because if you call the police station, they can verify that Jane had been living on the streets until recently. She was beaten up by Mark Adams and was a witness at his trial."

"Let me make a phone call to verify what you just said?" Mr. Oliver went to the phone on his secretary's desk and called the police station.

"Ask for Officer Bartlett, he talked to me at the hospital," Jane added.

Mr. Oliver hung up the phone after his conversation with the officer. "I was told you had a nervous breakdown shortly after your father died and you were in a home receiving treatment. I didn't investigate because I knew how close you were with your father and she showed me commitment papers. Your stepmother always seemed so concerned for your welfare...."

Suddenly, Jane jumped up and started vomiting violently into the waste basket beside the desk.

"Call 911," Sarah yelled. "She has been sick all night. Something is not right."

Ten minutes later, the paramedics arrived and took over. They got Jane on a stretcher and gave her fluids as they headed for the hospital. Mr. Oliver and Sarah followed in his car.

When they arrived, Dr. O'Brien was already examining Jane in the emergency ward. Mr. Oliver handed the letter to him and the lock of hair, as they had a short conversation just outside the exam room. An hour later, Jane went into labour. Sarah remembered her coaching giving her ice chips, wiping her face and neck with a wet wash cloth, and rubbing her back. When the pains came, she did the breathing exercises with her and offered her hand to be squeezed. When the baby was born, she was small and very delicate looking. She was red and wrinkly. Jane hardly got to see her before the nurses whisked her away.

"Where are they taking her? I am keeping my baby," Jane cried out as she disappeared through the door in a nurse's arms.

"Jane, it is all right. I have ordered some tests be done on the baby. The same ones you are about to have. I want to make sure you are both healthy," Dr. O'Brien said through his white mask. He then took a vial of blood from Jane's arm. "They are going to move you into your room and the baby will be with you shortly. Sarah stay with her and if she starts vomiting again, call a nurse immediately."

Jane had just settled into her new room and Sarah was sitting in a chair near the bed when the baby in an incubator was wheeled in and put right beside Jane's bed. She had a few tubes in her that the nurse explained was giving her medicine and fluids. The girls had never seen such a small baby. The baby had a blindfold covering her eyes which the nurse had said was to protect her eyes from the light they had shining on her. It was to help her from getting jaundice. When Jane reached in and touched her daughter's hand, the baby grabbed it and held on tight.

Dr. O'Brien came into the room and sat down beside Jane's bed. "We have the results. You were being given increasing doses of arsenic. I am giving you sulphur, and you are going to be on a high fibre diet for a while. We are treating the baby for arsenic poisoning as well. She is small but she is a fighter so I think she will be fine.
Are you up to talking with Mr. Oliver now?"

"Yes, have him come in."

"Sarah, I want you to stay with these two. If they show any breathing distress or vomiting, call a nurse immediately. I am going to have another bed moved in here. When is you due date?"

"It is three weeks away," Sarah said as she rubbed her belly where the baby had just kicked her.

"Your baby has dropped into position so you could have the baby anytime now," the doctor said as he left the room.

"I will let you talk to him alone," Sarah said as she got up to leave as Mr. Oliver entered the room.

"No, Sarah, he can talk to me in front of you. If it wasn't for you, my baby and I could be dead somewhere. I can't thank you enough." Jane said as she reached out and squeezed Sarah's hand.

"I have to ask you for permission to exhume your father's body. We must prove the hair you gave me came from your father. Dr. O'Brien has confirmed that the hair sample you gave me contained arsenic and that was what you have been given. We then will lay charges of murder and attempted murder against your mother. Sarah also said a man named Chuck was helping her. He will be charged also. In the meantime, we are putting all three of you under guard in this room. The police are looking for your step mother and Chuck now. They were not at the house when they got there this morning.

I must apologize to you. I didn't know that you were pregnant or that you were out living on the street. I just trusted what your mother said since I was not to tell you anything until your sixteenth birthday. I hope you forgive me," Mr. Oliver said as he dabbed his forehead with a handkerchief.

"I know it wasn't your fault. You were just following my mother's orders. She had no idea that father would marry someone like my stepmother. I still can't believe that she would try to harm me like she did," Jane said as she shook her head.

"Well since we have broken your mother's request already, I can tell you that you are a very wealthy lady. Your mother's estate consists of a large trust fund, a shoe company, and your house. When your parents died, they left everything to you in their wills. The only thing your stepmother got was insurance money. I wondered when your father changed his will three days before he died. Your mother was supposed to get the house and an allowance to live on for the rest of her life. She was livid when the will was read, and everything went to you."

"I bet," Jane chuckled. "Sarah, our problems are all solved. We have a house to raise our children in. There is furniture in it, so we only need baby items for their room. We have funds enough to pay for our schooling when the children are old enough to go to day care. This is great?" Jane smiled at Sarah.

"Jane, it is your money not mine," Sarah said.

"You saved me and my baby and believed in me when I doubted my own sanity. I can at least pay you back by paying for your schooling," Jane and Sarah both sat with tears streaming down their faces.

The next day, Sarah had her little girl. They all stayed in the hospital until Dr. O'Brien was sure that Jane and her baby where on the mend.

Mr. Oliver had taken over and hired a decorator to set up a nursery for the girls and removing her stepmother's furniture and replacing it with the furniture Jane grew up with. He even met them at their hospital room the day they were leaving the hospital with two baby car seats and outfits for each baby to come home in. Each girl prepared their daughters to go home.

On the drive home, he told them that Jane's father had been exhumed and he had been poisoned with arsenic. Chuck and Helen had been arrested trying to flee the country. They would be facing murder and attempted murder charges.

CHAPTER 21

Mr. Oliver had given the girls an allowance to live on until Jane was sixteen. Today was her birthday so he was going to her house to have her sign a bunch of papers. He felt a bit unsure about turning such a large sum of money over to a young girl who had no parental guidance.

When he entered the house, he was surprised. Everything was neat and clean. The air was filled with the smell of baking and the babied were both being fed when he entered.

"This is very nice and homey," Mr. Oliver said.

"Jane and I have been busy setting up things," Sarah said.

"What things," asked Mr. Oliver

"Jane got all the bills changed over to her name. We calculated how much it is to run the house. I am on Social Assistance, so I pay Jane rent equal to half of the expenses plus an emergency fund we set up. We opened a joint account to pay these bills. We each have our own savings and checking accounts for our personal expenses. The insurance man was here and we both have life insurance and Jane has house insurance. I think we have done everything we need to do," said Sarah.

"There is one more thing," Jane said as she burped her baby and continued rocking her. "We need to make an appointment with you to get our wills made."

"We can do them now after you sign these papers."

Mr. Oliver explained what she was signing and where she was to sign as they went page by page of the document he had taken out of his briefcase.

"You are now the majority owner of a shoe company. I realize that you may not want that responsibility right now, but I will advise you until you learn the business. I think from the looks of what you girls have accomplished so far you won't need my help for long." "We were just following our list," Jane smiled.

"List," questioned the lawyer.

"When we decided in the hospital that we were going to live together and help each other accomplish our dreams, we made a list of the things we needed to do. We asked the nurses, Dr. O'Brien, and our counsellors for their suggestions and made a list." Jane said as she rocked her sleeping baby.

Mr. Oliver got his notepad out so he could write down what they wanted in their wills. They gave the guardianship of their babies to each other and any inheritance to their own child. They also asked him if he could think of anything else that they had missed.

"Did you insure the babies' lives and set up college funds for them?"

"We did," Sarah said.

"Then I think you both did a wonderful job of preparing for the future of your families."

"Would you like to see the rest of the house," Jane asked feeling proud of what she had accomplished.

"Yes, I would." Mr. Oliver said as he followed the girls into the open concept kitchen/dining room. The modern furniture had been replaced by her father's wooden table and chairs he had made years before.

"This has all been renovated," Mr. Oliver said as he looked over the kitchen area.

"My stepmother did this with the money you had given her."

"At least you got some of the money back that I gave her. It also raises the value of your house."

"We want to thank you for getting the nursery set up for us while we were in the hospital," Jane said as they entered the nursery. "It was nice coming home to a clean house with it set up the way we wanted it. We love the murals and letters the decorator put in this room."

"I had to pay you back somehow for the mistake I made in trusting your stepmother," Mr. Oliver said.

"We all trusted her that was the problem." Jane said as she thought about her father.

The girls put their babies in their cribs and covered them. Jane turned on classical music and told Mr. Oliver, "Classical music is supposed to be good for them. They sure enjoy sleeping with it playing."

"You girls amaze me. You have thought out everything that you need to succeed and raise you family into a stable home.

"We work as a team," Sarah said smiling at Jane.

"I can see you both getting your education and working at the jobs you love. Jane, your parents would be very proud of you," Mr. Oliver said as he left the house with a smile on his face.

www.ingramcontent.com/pod-product-compliance
Lightning Source LLC
Chambersburg PA
CBHW031252210726
48287CB00003B/1005